John Milton, C. P. Mason

Books I. and II. of Milton's Paradise Lost

with notes on the analysis, and on the scriptural and classical allusions

John Milton, C. P. Mason

Books I. and II. of Milton's Paradise Lost
with notes on the analysis, and on the scriptural and classical allusions

ISBN/EAN: 9783337094232

Printed in Europe, USA, Canada, Australia, Japan

Cover: Foto ©Andreas Hilbeck / pixelio.de

More available books at **www.hansebooks.com**

Miller & Co.'s Educational Series.

BOOKS I. AND II.

OF

MILTON'S PARADISE LOST,

WITH

Notes on the Analysis, and on the Scriptural and Classical Allusions,

A GLOSSARY OF DIFFICULT WORDS.

AND A

LIFE OF MILTON.

BY

C. P. MASON, B.A., F.C.P.,

FELLOW OF UNIVERSITY COLLEGE, LONDON.

FIFTH EDITION.

TORONTO:
ADAM MILLER & CO.,
1878.

PREFACE.

THE favourable reception which the first edition of this little work met with has emboldened me to republish it for the use of candidates at the next Oxford Local Examinations. The alterations in the notes will not be found to be very numerous. They consist chiefly in corrections of the account given of adverbial sentences beginning with *as*, in accordance with the view of the matter set forth in the last edition of my English Grammar, and in my "Analysis of Sentences applied to Latin."

The first book of Milton's "Paradise Lost" is long and difficult. The style is intricate, and it is crowded with allusions to the Scriptures and to classical mythology. It is not a subject that can be hurried over, and those who have to prepare for examination in it will find the advantage of the longer notice of the subjects for examination which has been given by the Oxford Delegacy.

C. P. MASON.

DENMARK HILL,
July, 1870.

LIFE OF MILTON.

John Milton was the son of John and Sarah Milton, and was born Dec. 9, 1608, in Bread-street, where his father carried on the profession of a scrivener. The latter was a man of good family, the son of a yeoman of Oxfordshire, but had been disinherited on account of his Protestantism. He had been educated at Christchurch, Oxford, and was besides a man of great musical taste and acquirements. From him Milton inherited that musical taste which in later life provided him with a solace for many weary hours. Milton's early years were passed amid the influences of an orderly and pious Puritan household. His first teacher was a Scotchman, named Thomas Young. While still under his care he was sent to St. Paul's School, the head-master of which was Alexander Gill, who was assisted by his son of the same name. While here, Milton was a hard student, and already began to exert his poetical powers. His versions of the 114th and 136th Psalms were composed in his sixteenth year. On the 12th of February, 1624,* Milton was admitted as a lesser pensioner at Christ's College, Cambridge. With his first tutor, William Chappell, Milton had some variance, which led to the interference of the college authorities, in consequence of which Milton was rusticated for a short time, but soon returned, and was transferred to the tutorship of the Rev. Nathaniel Tovey. There is a statement (the authenticity of which, however, is disputed) that Milton's quarrel with his tutor brought on him the indignity of a whipping. There is nothing, however, to show that this was anything more than a private *fracas.* Milton's rather haughty and fastidious manners at first made him the object of some dislike; but long before he left college he had won the favour and respect of his college, and of the whole university. He took his B.A. degree in January, 1628 (1629), and his M.A.

* Before 1752 the year was reckoned to begin on the 25th of March. According to our present mode of reckoning the above date would be Feb. 12, 1625.

degree in July, 1632. He was at first designed for the Church, and went through the usual course of theological study; but he also pursued with great assiduity an independent course of his own. He was especially noted for the excellence of his Latin versification. While at college he wrote, in Latin, the first four of his *Familiar Epistles;* seven college themes, published in 1674, under the title of *Prolusiones quædam Oratoriæ;* the *Elegiarum Liber;* and part of the *Sylvarum Liber.* In English he wrote various minor poems:—1. "On the Death of a Fair Infant." 2. "Part of a Vacation Exercise." 3. "On Time." 4. "On the Circumcision." 5. "At a Solemn Music." 6. "On May Morning." 7. "On Shakspere." 8. "On the University Carrier." 9. "Epitaph on the Marchioness of Winchester." 10. "Sonnet on my Twenty-third Birthday." The epitaph on Shakspere was the only one of these compositions which was published during his stay at college. It appeared anonymously among the laudatory verses prefixed to the second folio edition of Shakspere in 1632, and was the first of Milton's productions which appeared in print.

On leaving college Milton declined both the Church and the Bar, and spent the ensuing five years at Horton, in Buckinghamshire, at the residence of his father, who had retired from business with a competent fortune. These years were spent in fruitful study, and occasional literary labours. It was during this period that he wrote "L'Allegro" and "Il Penseroso," "Arcades," "Comus," and "Lycidas," a monody on the death of Mr. Edward King, who had been his companion at college.

Milton's mother died in 1637, and soon after he obtained leave and means from his father to make a continental tour, in the course of which he visited Paris and most of the chief cities in Italy, and made acquaintance with Grotius, Galileo, and Manso, the friend and patron of Tasso. He had intended continuing his journey to Greece, but the news which reached him of impending civil commotions in England induced him to return. This Italian journey, and the reputation and praise which he gained in literary circles, greatly stimulated his literary ambition. But his purpose of writing some great English poem was interrupted by the outbreak of the civil war, which diverted his energies into a totally new channel. Milton was heart and soul a Republican and an Independent, and devoted his genius and energy to the cause of the revolution. For the next twenty years his poetical efforts were relinquished, and we see him only as the most masterly polemical prose writer of his age.

On his return to England, Milton found the household at Horton broken up, and went (in 1640) to reside in St. Bride's Churchyard, Fleet-street; whence he removed (in 1641) to a house in Aldersgate-street, where he took some pupils to educate, with his nephews, Edward and John Phillips. In 1641 he began his political career by a vigorous attack on prelacy, in a treatise entitled, "Of Reformation touching Church Discipline in England, and the Causes that hitherto have hindered it." A reply to this was published by Bishop Hall, who, in his turn, was answered in a work which was the joint production of five Puritan ministers—Stephen Marshall, Edward Calamy, Thomas Young, Matthew Newcomen, and William Spurstow, whose joint initials made up the name "Smectymnuus." This work called forth a reply from Archbishop Usher, upon which Milton came to the rescue with his pamphlets entitled, "Of Prelatical Episcopacy," and "The Reason of Church Government urged against Prelacy." Other publications of Milton's in this controversy were, "Animadversions upon the Remonstrant's Defence," and "The Apology against a Pamphlet called, 'A Modest Confutation of the Animadversions upon the Remonstrant against Smectymnuus.'"

In 1643 Milton took a short journey into the country, in the course of which he married Mary, the eldest daughter of Mr. Richard Powell, of Forest Hill, near Shotover, in Oxfordshire. Mrs. Milton, however, whose mind and tastes were utterly uncongenial to those of her husband, found or fancied her married life unbearable, and having gone home for a visit, refused to return. Milton accordingly repudiated her, and the quarrel led to the publication of his four treatises on divorce, in which he maintained that moral incompatibility is as good a ground for divorce as conjugal infidelity. In 1645, however, his wife's family brought about a reconciliation, and she returned to her husband, who had now taken a house in Barbican, where his aged father was residing with him. It was in 1644 that Milton wrote his "Tractate on Education," and his noble "Areopagitica; or, Speech for the Liberty of Unlicensed Printing," in defence of the freedom of the press. In 1645 he published, in a small volume, the first edition of his minor poems.

On the capture of Oxford by the Parliamentary army, in 1646, Mrs. Milton's father and his family were driven from home, and took refuge in Milton's house, where, not long after, Mr. Powell died. Milton's eldest daughter, Anne, was born in 1646, and his aged father died soon after. In 1647, the Powells having returned to Oxfordshire, and the number of his pupils having fallen off, Milton removed to a smaller house in Holborn, where he employed himself in study and writing. About this time he produced a portion of his "History of England."

On the execution of Charles I. (Jan. 30, 1648-9), Milton published, in justification of the act, a short pamphlet, "On the Tenure of Kings and Magistrates." This led to his receiving from the Government the offer of the post of Latin or Foreign Secretary, which he accepted, with a salary of £290 per annum. He now removed to an official residence in the neighbourhood of Whitehall. In the early part of this year he also published "Animadversions on the Articles of Peace between the Earl of Ormond and the Irish Rebels." His next important work was the "Eikonoklastes," written in 1649, in answer to the celebrated "Eikon Basilike." This had scarcely been completed, when Salmasius (Claude de Saumaise), at the instigation of Charles II., then a refugee in Holland, published his "Defensio Regia pro Carolo Primo ad Carolum Secundum." At the request of the English Council of State, Milton wrote in reply his famous "Defensio pro Populo Anglicano contra Claudii anonymi alias Salmasii Defensionem Regiam," which was published in 1650, by order of the Council. The preparation of this work was believed by Milton himself to have hastened the calamitous failure of his sight, of which symptoms had appeared in 1644, and which, by the year 1653, resulted in total blindness, from the affection termed *gutta serena*. Notwithstanding his blindness, he continued to fulfil the duties of his office nearly up to the time of the Restoration. During the latter part of this period he was assisted by his friend Andrew Marvell. In 1654, he published his "Defensio Secunda pro Populo Anglicano," in reply to a scurrilous production by Peter Dumoulin, the reputed author of which at the time was Alexander More. This was followed up by his "Authoris pro se Defensio contra Alexandrum Morum Ecclesiastem" (1655), and "Authoris ad Alexandri Mori Supplementum Defensio" (1655). In addition to these works he produced in his official capacity between seventy and eighty Latin letters, and a Latin State Paper on the differences of the Protector with the Spanish Court. His last official letter is dated May 15, 1659. In this year he wrote two tracts addressed to the Parliament, "A Treatise of Civil Power in Ecclesiastical Causes," and "Considerations touching the likeliest means to remove Hirelings out of the Church," and also a "Letter to a Friend, concerning the Ruptures of the Commonwealth," and "The Ready and Easy Way to establish a Free Commonwealth." These treatises were all intended to stem the reaction in favour of royalty and high-church principles. On the restoration of Charles II. (1660) Milton was for some time in considerable danger. His most obnoxious writings were burnt by the hangman. He was in custody, after the passing of the Act of Indemnity, and is said to have owed his safety to the intercession of Sir William Davenant, who at an earlier period had been beholden to Milton for his good offices when taken prisoner at sea.

In November, 1656, Milton had married his second wife, Catherine Woodcock, who died in childbirth, about a year afterwards. In the early part of 1663 he married his third wife, Elizabeth Minshull. The relations of his daughters towards their step-mother were not of the happiest kind, and the two elder in particular were also unkind and undutiful to their father, whom they cheated and robbed. He employed his two younger daughters in writing at his dictation, and reading to him in several languages, without understanding their meaning, a kind of work with which they appear to have become utterly disgusted. All three were at last sent from home to gain their own livelihood. Though no longer in affluent circumstances, Milton still retained enough of the property bequeathed to him by his father to enable him to live, in his frugal way, in tolerable ease and comfort. During the latter part of his life he resided in Artillery Walk. The following are the prose works which belong to the later period of his life. 1. "Accidence commenced Grammar." 2. "The History of Britain." 3. "Artis Logicæ plenior Institutio." 4. "Of True Religion, Heresie, Schism, and Toleration." 5. "Epistolarum Familiarum liber unus, quibus accesserunt Prolusiones quædam Oratoriæ." 6. "A Brief History of Moscovia." 7. "A Treatise (in Latin) on Christian Doctrine." The publication of this work, in which Milton's Arian creed was developed, was given up by his friends, on prudential grounds. The manuscript of it was discovered in 1823, in the State Paper Office. In the reading and writing which his literary labours involved, Milton had the help of various voluntary assistants, besides his daughters, particularly that of a young Quaker, named Ellwood.

It was in these later years of blindness, poverty, and affliction, that the genius of Milton reverted to its original bent. With a mind stored with learning, and strengthened and refined by the vast experience of twenty years of active participation in the noble struggle by which freedom was won; with a fancy chastened by age and purified by suffering; and with an imagination unsurpassed in the sublimity of its range, and intensified by the very affliction which cut it off from all sources of inspiration but those which it created for itself, Milton addressed himself to the composition of his immortal poem, "Paradise Lost." This work was finished by 1665, in which year it was shown to Ellwood; but it was not till April 27th, 1667 that it was sold to Samuel Simmons, the publisher, for £5 down with a promise of £5 more when 1,300 copies of the first edition should have been sold, £5 more when 1,300 copies of the second edition should have been sold, and so on; each edition to consist of 1,500 copies. It was two years before Milton received the second £5. The second edition was not published till 1674, the year of Milton's death. A third edition was published in 1678, and in 1680 Milton's widow sold her interest in the book for £8. In the second edition the original ten books were made into twelve, by a division of the seventh and tenth books.

The poem, "Paradise Regained," was suggested to Milton by a question put to him one day by Ellwood. It was published in 1671, together with "Samson Agonistes."

Milton died November 8th, 1674, and was buried in the chancel of St. Giles, Cripplegate. In stature he was somewhat below the average. In his youth he was singularly handsome, with an appearance of almost feminine grace and delicacy. In his old age, in addition to his blindness, he suffered from gout and other infirmities. His wife survived him for forty-five years, and died, at a great age, at Nantwich. His brother Christopher adhered steadily to the royalist party. He was knighted by James II., and became a judge.

EXAMPLES OF THE ANALYSIS OF SENTENCES.

In analysing sentences proceed in the following manner:—

1. Set down the subject of the sentence, which may consist (1) of a single substantive, or (2) of two or more substantives united by co-ordinative conjunctions, or (3) of an infinitive mood, or (4) of a quotation, or (5) of a subordinate substantive clause.

2. Set down the attributive adjuncts of the subject. These may consist (1) of an adjective or participle (with or without adjuncts of their own), or (2) of a noun (or a substantive clause) in apposition to the subject, or (3) of a substantive (noun or pronoun) in the possessive case, or (4) of a substantive preceded by a preposition (including under this head an infinitive mood preceded by *to*), or (5) of an adjective clause.

3. Set down the predicate-verb. If the verb is one of incomplete predication, set down the complement of the predicate, and indicate that the verb and its complement make up the entire predicate.

4. If the predicate be a transitive verb, set down the object of the verb. The object of a verb admits of the same varieties as the subject. If the predicate be a verb of incomplete predication, followed by an infinitive mood, set down the object of the dependent infinitive.

5. Set down those words, phrases, or adjective clauses, which are in the attributive relation to the object of the predicate, or to the object of the complement of the predicate, if the latter be a verb in the infinitive mood.

6. Set down those words, phrases, or adverbial clauses which are in the adverbial relation to the predicate. These adverbial adjuncts may consists (1) of an adverb; or (2) of a substantive (or verb in the infinitive mood) preceded by a preposition; or (3) of a noun qualified by an attributive word; or (4) of a substantive (noun or pronoun) in the objective case, before which *to* or *for* may be understood; or (5) of a nominative absolute; or (6) of an adverbial clause.

7. Set down the adverbial adjuncts of the complement of the predicate.

8. Analyse the subordinate clauses which enter into the construction of the principal sentence.

A. "What man that lives, and that knows how to live, would fail to exhibit at the public shows a form as splendid as the proudest there."

Analysis of A.

Subject, 'man.'

Attrib. adjuncts of subject,
1. 'What.'
2. *Adjective clause*, 'that lives.' (B.)
3. *Adjective clause*, 'that knows how to live.' (C.)

Predicate (incomplete), 'would fail.'
Complement of predicate, 'to exhibit.'
Object of the complement, 'form.'

Attrib. adjuncts of object,
1. 'a.'
2. 'splendid,' *qualified by* (1) 'as — (2) as the proudest there.' (D.)

Adverbial adjunct of complement of predicate, 'at the public shows.'

Analysis of B.

Subject, 'that.'
Predicate, 'lives.'

Analysis of C.

Subject, 'that.'
Predicate, 'knows.'
Object, 'to live.'
Adverbial adjunct of object, 'how.'

Analysis of D.

In full: 'As [the form is splendid which] the proudest there [exhibit].'
Subject, 'form.'

Attrib. adjuncts of subject,
1. *Article*, 'the.'
2. *Adjective clause*, 'which the proudest there exhibit.' (E.)

Predicate,
Verb of incomplete predication, 'is.'
Complement of predicate, 'splendid.'

Adverbial adjunct of the complement of the predicate, 'as.'

Analysis of E.

Subject, 'persons' (understood).

Attrib. adjuncts of subject,
1. *Article*, 'the.'
2. *Adjective*, 'proudest.'
3. *Adverb*, 'there' (*Gr.* 362*).

Predicate, 'exhibit.'
Object, 'which.'

"Our habits, costlier than Lucullus wore,
And by caprice as multiplied as his,
Just please us while the fashion is at full."

Subject, 'habits.'

Attrib. adjuncts of subject,
1. 'Our.'
2. 'costlier than Lucullus wore.' (B.)
3. 'by caprice as multiplied as his.' (C.)

Predicate, 'please.'
Object, 'us.'

Adverbial adjuncts of predicate,
1. 'just.'
2. *Adverbial clause*, 'while the fashion is at full.' (D.)

Analysis of B.

An adverbial clause, qualifying *costlier*. In full: 'Than the habits were costly which Lucullus wore.'

Subject, 'habits.'

Attrib. adjuncts of subject,
1. 'the.'
2. *Adjective clause*, 'which Lucullus wore. (E.)

Predicate,
Verb of incomplete predication, 'were.'
Complement of predicate, 'costly.'

Adverbial adjunct of complement of predicate, 'than.'

Analysis of E.

Subject, 'Lucullus.'
Predicate, 'wore.'
Object, 'which.'

Analysis of C.

An elliptical adverbial clause co-ordinate with *as* which qualifies *multiplied.* In full: 'As his habits were multiplied.'

Subject, 'habits.'

Attributive adjunct of subject, 'his.'

Predicate, { *Verb of incomplete predication,* 'were.' / *Complement,* 'multiplied.

Adverbial adjunct of complement, 'as.'

Analysis of D.

'While the fashion is at full.'

Subject, 'fashion.'

Attributive adjunct of subject, 'the.'

Predicate, 'is.'

Adverbial adjuncts of predicate, { 1. 'while.' / 2. 'at full.'

"Too well I see, and rue the dire event,
That with sad overthrow, and foul defeat,
Hath lost us heaven, and all this mighty host
In horrible destruction laid thus low,
As far as gods and heavenly essences
Can perish."

At full length: A. "Too well I see the dire event that——heaven, and that all this——low, as far as gods and heavenly essences can perish [far]." B. "And I rue the dire event," &c.

Analysis of A.

Subject, 'I.'

Predicate, 'see.'

Object, 'event.'

Attributive adjuncts of object,
1. 'the.'
2. 'dire.'
3. *Adjective clause:* 'That with sad —— heaven.' (C.)
4. *Adjective clause:* 'That all this mighty ——can perish.' (D.)

Adverbial adjunct of predicate, 'too well.'

Analysis of C.

Subject, 'that.'

Predicate, 'hath lost.

Object, 'heaven.'

Adverbial adjuncts of object, { 1. 'with sad overthrow.' 2. 'with foul defeat.' 3. 'us' (*i.e.*, 'for us').

Analysis of D.

Subject, 'that.'

Predicate, { *Verb of incomplete predication*, 'hath laid.' *Complement of predicate*, 'low.'

Object, 'host.'

Attributive adjuncts of object, { 1. 'all.' 2. 'this.' 3. 'mighty.'

Adverbial adjuncts of predicate, { 1. 'In horrible destruction.' 2. 'As far as gods and heavenly essences can perish.' (E.)

Adverbial adjunct of the complement of the predicate, 'thus.'

Analysis of E.

"As gods and heavenly essences can perish [far]." An adverbial clause, co-ordinate with *as* which qualifies *far*.

Subject (compound), 'gods and essences.'

Attributive adjunct of part of subject, 'heavenly.'

Predicate, { *Verb of incomplete predication*, 'can.' *Complement*, 'perish.'

Adverbial adjunct of predicate, 'far' (understood), which is itself qualified by the relative adverb *as*.

The analysis of B is step for step the same as that of A, with the substitution of *rue* for *see*.

"Blest he, though undistinguished from the crowd
By wealth or dignity, who dwells secure,
Where man, by nature fierce, has laid aside
His fierceness, having learnt, though slow to learn,
The manners and the arts of civil life."

At full length: A. "Blest is he, though he be undistinguished from the crowd by wealth, who dwells, &c.——life." B. "Blest is he, though he be undistinguished from the crowd by dignity, who dwells——life."

Analysis of A.

Subject, 'he.'

Attrib. adjunct of subject, { *Adjective clause*, 'who dwells secure where ——life.' (C.)

Predicate (*incomplete*), 'is.'
Complement of predicate, 'blest.'
Adverbial adjunct of predicate, { *Clause*, 'though he be undistinguished—— wealth.' (D.)

Analysis of C.

Subject, 'who.'
Predicate, 'dwells.'
Complement of predicate, 'secure.'
Adverbial adjunct of predicate, { *Adverbial clause*, 'where man by——life.' (E.)

Analysis of E.

Subject, 'man.'
Attrib. adjuncts of subject, { 1. *Adjective phrase*, 'by nature fierce.' 2. *Participial phrase*, 'having learnt, though *he is slow* to learn——life.' (F.)
Predicate, 'has laid.'
Object of verb, 'fierceness.'
Attributive adjunct of object, 'his.'
Adverbial adjuncts of predicate, { 1. 'aside.' 2. 'where.'

Analysis of F.

'[Though] he is slow to learn.'
Subject, 'he.'
Predicate (*incomplete*), 'is.'
Complement of predicate, 'slow.'
Adverbial adjunct of complement of predicate, 'to learn.'

Analysis of D.

Subject, 'he.'
Predicate incomplete, 'be.'
Complement of predicate, 'undistinguished.'
Adverbial adjuncts of complement of predicate, { 1. 'from the crowd.' 2. 'by wealth.'

Analysis of B.

The analysis of B is step for step the same as that of A, with the substitution of *dignity* for *wealth*.

The *parsing* of a sentence takes cognizance of more minute particulars than the above kind of analysis. A specimen of the mode in which it is to be conducted is given in the *Grammar*, p. 143.

The following is the mode in which the preceding sentences would be bracketed and marked, according to the method* set forth in the author's English Grammar, § 507.

A. "What man (a'_1. that lives) and (a'_2. that knows how to live), would fail to exhibit at the public shows a form as splendid {c''. as the proudest there."}

B. "Our habits costlier {a''. than† ($a''b'$. Lucullus wore)}, and by caprice as multiplied {c''. as his}, just please us {d''. while the fashion is at full."}

C. "Too well I see, and rue the dire event (a'_1. that with sad overthrow and foul defeat hath lost us heaven) and (a'_2. [that] all this mighty host in horrible destruction [hath] laid thus low as far {a'_2b''. as gods and heavenly essences can perish."})

D. "Blest he, {m''. though undistinguished from the crowd by wealth or dignity} [n'. who dwells secure {$n'o''$. where man, by nature fierce, has laid aside his fierceness, having learnt ($n'o''p''$. though slow to learn) the manners and the arts of civil life."}]

The following examples will still further illustrate the method :—

E. {a''_1. "Me though just right, and the fixed laws of heaven, did first create your leader,} {a''_2 next free choice, with (a''_2b' what besides in counsel, or in fight, hath been achieved of merit) *did create your leader,*} yet this loss, thus far at least recovered, hath much more established *me* in a safe unenvied throne, yielded with full consent."

F. "Who here will envy *him* (a'_1. whom the highest place exposes foremost to stand against the Thunderer's aim your bulwark), and (a'_2. *whom the highest place* condemns to greatest share of endless pain ?) {b''. Where there is then no good ($b''c'$. for which *we need* to strive,)} no strife can grow up there from faction ; {d''_1. for none sure will claim in hell precedence,} {d''_2. *for there is none* (d''_2e'. whose portion is so small of present pain,) (d''_2f'. that with ambitious mind will covet more.")}

---

* The slightly modified method adopted in the sixteenth edition is here referred to.

† In full {a''. than the habits ($a''b'$. which Lucullus wore) were costly}.

G. "Let such bethink them {a''. if the sleepy drench of that forgetful lake benumb not still,} [b_1. that in our proper motion we ascend up to our native seat:] [b_2. descent and fall to us is adverse."]

H. "Who *was there* but (a'. *who* felt of late {$a'b''_1$. when the fierce foe hung on our broken rear insulting,} {$a'b''_2$ and *when the fierce foe* pursued us through the deep,} [$a'c$. with what compulsion and laborious flight we sunk thus low?"])

I. "What can be worse {a''. than to dwell here, driven out from bliss, condemned in this abhorred deep to utter woe, ($a''b'$. where pain of unextinguishable fire must exercise us without hope of end, the vassals of his anger, [$a''b'c''$. when the scourge inexorable and the torturing hour calls us to penance?"])}.

K. "I should be much for open war, O peers, {a''. as *I am* not behind in hate,} {b''_1. if ($b''c'$ what was urged main reason to persuade immediate war) did not dissuade me most,} and {b''_2. *if* (b''_2c'. *what was urged main reason to persuade immediate war*) did not seem to cast ominous conjecture on the whole success, [$b_2''d''$. when he ($b''_2d''e'$. who most excels in feats of arms) in ($b''_2d''f'$. what he counsels) and in *that* ($b''_2d''g'$. *in which he* excels,) mistrustful grounds his courage on despair and utter dissolution ($b''_2d''h''$. as *he would ground his courage on* the scope of all his aim, after some dire revenge.")]}

In the following example, which contains several principal sentences, the subordinate clauses of each are distinguished from those of the others by having the signature of the complete sentence prefixed to that of each subordinate clause.

A. "There is a place {Aa''. if ancient and prophetic fame in heaven err not,} another world, the happy seat of some new race, called Man, about this time to be created, like to us, {Ab''. though less in power and excellence}, but favoured more of him (Ac'. who rules above). *B*. So was his will pronounced among the gods; *C*. and by an oath (Ca'. that shook heaven's whole circumference) confirmed. *D*. Thither let us bend all our thoughts, to learn [Db_1. what creatures there inhabit], [Db_2. of what mould] or [Db_3. substance,] [Db_4. how endued] and [Db_5. what their power."]

PARADISE LOST.

BOOK I.

Of Man's first disobedience, and the fruit
Of that forbidden tree, whose mortal taste
Brought death into the world, and all our woe,
With loss of Eden, till one greater man
Restore us, and regain the blissful seat,
Sing, heavenly muse, that on the secret top
Of Oreb, or of Sinai, didst inspire
That Shepherd who first taught the chosen seed,
In the beginning how the heavens and earth
Rose out of chaos: or if Sion's hill
Delight thee more, and Siloa's brook that flow'd
Fast by the oracle of God, I thence
Invoke thy aid to my adventurous song,
That with no middle flight intends to soar
Above the Aonian mount, while it pursues
Things unattempted yet in prose or rhyme.
And chiefly thou, O Spirit, that dost prefer
Before all temples the upright heart and pure,
Instruct me, for thou know'st; thou from the first
Wast present, and, with mighty wings outspread,
Dove-like sat'st brooding on the vast abyss,
And madest it pregnant: what in me is dark,
Illumine: what is low, raise and support;
That to the height of this great argument
I may assert eternal Providence,

And justify the ways of God to men.
  Say first—for Heaven hides nothing from thy view,
Nor the deep tract of hell—say first what cause
Moved our grand parents, in that happy state,
Favour'd of Heaven so highly to fall off
From their Creator, and transgress his will
For one restraint, lords of the world besides.
Who first seduced them to that foul revolt?
The infernal serpent; he it was, whose guile,
Stirr'd up with envy and revenge, deceived
The mother of mankind, what time his pride
Had cast him out from heaven, with all his host
Of rebel angels; by whose aid aspiring
To set himself in glory above his peers,
He trusted to have equalled the Most High,
If he opposed; and with ambitious aim
Against the throne and monarchy of God,
Raised impious war in heaven, and battle proud,
With vain attempt. Him the Almighty Power
Hurl'd headlong flaming from the ethereal sky,
With hideous ruin and combustion down
To bottomless perdition, there to dwell
In adamantine chains and penal fire,
Who durst defy the Omnipotent to arms.
Nine times the space that measures day and night
To mortal men, he with his horrid crew
Lay vanquish'd rolling in the fiery gulf,
Confounded, though immortal: but his doom
Reserved him to more wrath; for now the thought
Both of lost happiness and lasting pain
Torments him: round he throws his baleful eyes,
That witness'd huge affliction and dismay,
Mix'd with obdurate pride and stedfast hate.
At once as far as angels ken he views
The dismal situation waste and wild;
A dungeon horrible on all sides round

As one great furnace flamed; yet from those flames
No light; but rather darkness visible
Served only to discover sights of woe,
Regions of sorrow, doleful shades, where peace
And rest can never dwell, hope never comes,
That comes to all, but torture without end
Still urges, and a fiery deluge, fed
With ever-burning sulphur unconsumed.
Such place eternal Justice had prepared
For those rebellious: here their prison ordain'd
In utter darkness, and their portion set
As far removed from God and light of heaven,
As from the centre thrice to the utmost pole.
O, how unlike the place from whence they fell!
There the companions of his fall, o'erwhelmed
With floods and whirlwinds of tempestuous fire,
He soon discerns; and weltering by his side
One next himself in power, and next in crime,
Long after known in Palestine, and named
Beelzebub. To whom the arch-enemy,
And thence in heaven call'd Satan, with bold words
Breaking the horrid silence, thus began:
"If thou beest he; but O, how fall'n! how changed
From him who in the happy realms of light,
Clothed with transcendent brightness, didst outshine
Myriads though bright! If he, whom mutual league,
United thoughts and counsels, equal hope
And hazard in the glorious enterprise,
Join'd with me once, now misery hath join'd
In equal ruin: into what pit thou seest,
From what height fall'n, so much the stronger proved
He with his thunder: and till then who knew
The force of those dire arms? Yet not for those,
Nor what the potent Victor in his rage
Can else inflict, do I repent or change,
Though changed in outward lustre, that fix'd mind,

And high disdain from sense of injured merit,
That with the Mightiest raised me to contend,
And to the fierce contention brought along
Innumerable force of spirits arm'd
That durst dislike his reign, and, me preferring,
His utmost power with adverse power opposed
In dubious battle on the plains of heaven,
And shook his throne. What though the field be lost?
All is not lost; the unconquerable will,
And study of revenge, immortal hate,
And courage never to submit or yield,
And what is else not to be overcome:
That glory never shall his wrath or might
Extort from me. To bow and sue for grace
With suppliant knee, and deify his power
Who from the terror of this arm so late
Doubted his empire, that were low indeed,
That were an ignominy and shame beneath
This downfall: since by fate the strength of gods
And this empyreal substance cannot fail,
Since through experience of this great event
In arms not worse, in foresight much advanced,
We may with more successful hope resolve
To wage by force or guile eternal war,
Irreconcilable to our grand foe,
Who now triumphs, and, in the excess of joy
Sole reigning, holds the tyranny of heaven."
So spake the apostate angel, though in pain,
Vaunting aloud, but rack'd with deep despair:
And him thus answered soon his bold compeer:
"O prince, O chief of many throned powers,
That led the embattled seraphim to war
Under thy conduct, and in dreadful deeds
Fearless endanger'd heaven's perpetual King,
And put to proof his high supremacy,
Whether upheld by strength, or chance, or fate;

Too well I see, and rue the dire event,
That with sad overthrow, and foul defeat,
Hath lost us heaven, and all this mighty host
In horrible destruction laid thus low,
As far as gods and heavenly essences
Can perish: for the mind and spirit remain
Invincible, and vigour soon returns,
Though all our glory extinct, and happy state
Here swallowed up in endless misery.
But what if he our Conqueror (whom I now
Of force believe almighty, since no less
Than such could have o'erpower'd such force as ours,)
Have left us this our spirit and strength entire
Strongly to suffer and support our pains,
That we may so suffice his vengeful ire,
Or do him mightier service as his thralls
By right of war, whate'er his business be,
Here in the heart of hell to work in fire,
Or do his errands in the gloomy deep?
What can it then avail, though yet we feel
Strength undiminish'd, or eternal being
To undergo eternal punishment?"
Whereto with speedy words the arch-fiend replied:
"Fall'n cherub, to be weak is miserable
Doing or suffering; but of this be sure,
To do aught good never will be our task,
But ever to do ill our sole delight,
As being the contrary to his high will
Whom we resist. If then his providence
Out of our evil seek to bring forth good,
Our labour must be to pervert that end,
And out of good still to find means of evil,
Which ofttimes may succeed, so as perhaps
Shall grieve him, if I fail not, and disturb
His inmost counsels from their destined aim.
But see! the angry Victor hath recall'd

His ministers of vengeance and pursuit
Back to the gates of heaven: the sulphurous hail,
Shot after us in storm, o'erblown, hath laid
The fiery surge, that from the precipice
Of heaven received us falling; and the thunder,
Wing'd with red lightning and impetuous rage,
Perhaps hath spent his shafts, and ceases now
To bellow through the vast and boundless deep.
Let us not slip the occasion, whether scorn
Or satiate fury yield it from our foe.
Seest thou yon dreary plain, forlorn and wild,
The seat of desolation, void of light,
Save what the glimmering of these livid flames
Casts pale and dreadful? Thither let us tend
From off the tossing of these fiery waves;
There rest, if any rest can harbour there;
And, re-assembling our afflicted powers,
Consult how we may henceforth most offend
Our enemy; our own loss how repair;
How overcome this dire calamity;
What reinforcement we may gain from hope;
If not, what resolution from despair."
  Thus Satan talking to his nearest mate,
With head uplift above the wave, and eyes
That sparkling blazed: his other parts besides,
Prone on the flood extended long and large,
Lay floating many a rood; in bulk as huge
As whom the fables name of monstrous size,
Titanian, or Earth-born, that warr'd on Jove;
Briareus, or Typhon, whom the den
By ancient Tarsus held; or that sea-beast
Leviathan, which God of all his works
Created hugest that swim the ocean stream:
Him, haply slumbering on the Norway foam,
The pilot of some small night-founder'd skiff
Deeming some island, oft, as seamen tell,

With fixed anchor in his scaly rind
Moors by his side under the lee, while night
Invests the sea, and wished morn delays:
So stretch'd out huge in length the arch-fiend lay,
Chain'd on the burning lake: nor ever thence
Had risen or heaved his head, but that the will
And high permission of all-ruling Heaven
Left him at large to his own dark designs;
That with reiterated crimes he might
Heap on himself damnation, while he sought
Evil to others; and, enraged, might see
How all his malice served but to bring forth
Infinite goodness, grace, and mercy, shown
On man by him seduced; but on himself
Treble confusion, wrath, and vengeance pour'd.
Forthwith upright he rears from off the pool
His mighty stature; on each hand the flames,
Driven backward, slope their pointing spires, and roll'd
In billows, leave in the midst a horrid vale.
Then with expanded wings he steers his flight
Aloft, incumbent on the dusky air,
That felt unusual weight; till on dry land
He lights, if it were land that ever burn'd
With solid, as the lake with liquid fire:
And such appear'd in hue, as when the force
Of subterranean wind transports a hill
Torn from Pelorus, or the shatter'd side
Of thundering Ætna, whose combustible
And fuell'd entrails thence conceiving fire,
Sublimed with mineral fury, aid the winds,
And leave a singed bottom all involved
With stench and smoke: such resting found the sole
Of unblest feet. Him follow'd his next mate;
Both glorying to have 'scaped the Stygian flood
As gods, and by their own recovered strength,
Not by the sufferance of supernal power.

"Is this the region, this the soil, the clime,"
Said then the lost archangel, "this the seat
That we must change for heaven; this mournful gloom
For that celestial light? Be it so, since he,
Who now is Sovereign, can dispose and bid
What shall be right; farthest from him is best,
Whom reason hath equall'd, force hath made supreme
Above his equals. Farewell, happy fields,
Where joy for ever dwells! Hail horrors! hail
Infernal world! and thou profoundest hell,
Receive thy new possessor; one who brings
A mind not to be changed by place or time:
The mind is its own place, and in itself
Can make a heaven of hell, a hell of heaven.
What matter where, if I be still the same,
And what I should be—all but less than he
Whom thunder hath made greater? Here at least
We shall be free; the Almighty hath not built
Here for his envy, will not drive us hence:
Here we may reign secure, and, in my choice,
To reign is worth ambition, though in hell:
Better to reign in hell than serve in heaven.
But wherefore let we then our faithful friends,
The associates and copartners of our loss,
Lie thus astonish'd in the oblivious pool,
And call them not to share with us their part
In this unhappy mansion; or once more
With rallied arms to try what may be yet
Regain'd in heaven, or what more lost in hell?"
So Satan spake, and him Beelzebub
Thus answer'd: "Leader of those armies bright,
Which but the Omnipotent none could have foil'd,
If once they hear that voice, their liveliest pledge
Of hope in fears and dangers, heard so oft
In worst extremes, and on the perilous edge
Of battle when it raged, in all assaults

Their surest signal, they will soon resume
New courage and revive; though now they lie
Grovelling and prostrate on yon lake of fire,
As we erewhile, astounded and amazed;
No wonder, fall'n such a pernicious height."
He scarce had ceased when the superior fiend
Was moving toward the shore: his ponderous shield,
Ethereal temper, massy, large, and round,
Behind him cast: the broad circumference
Hung on his shoulders like the moon, whose orb
Through optic glass the Tuscan artist views
At evening from the top of Fesole,
Or in Valdarno, to descry new lands,
Rivers, or mountains, in her spotty globe.
His spear, to equal which the tallest pine
Hewn on Norwegian hills, to be the mast
Of some great ammiral, were but a wand,
He walk'd with, to support uneasy steps
Over the burning marle, not like those steps
On heaven's azure; and the torrid clime
Smote on him sore besides, vaulted with fire:
Nathless he so endured, till on the beach
Of that inflamed sea he stood, and call'd
His legions, angel forms, who lay entranced
Thick as autumnal leaves that strew the brooks
In Vallombrosa, where the Etrurian shades,
High over-arch'd, embower; or scatter'd sedge
Afloat, when with fierce winds Orion arm'd
Hath vex'd the Red Sea coast, whose waves o'erthrew
Busiris and his Memphian chivalry,
While with perfidious hatred they pursued
The sojourners of Goshen, who beheld
From the safe shore their floating carcases
And broken chariot-wheels: so thick bestrewn,
Abject and lost lay these, covering the flood,
Under amazement of their hideous change.

He call'd so loud, that all the hollow deep
Of hell resounded. "Princes, potentates,
Warriors, the flower of heaven, once yours, now lost,
If such astonishment as this can seize
Eternal spirits; or have ye chosen this place
After the toil of battle to repose
Your wearied virtue, for the ease you find
To slumber here, as in the vales of heaven?
Or in this abject posture have ye sworn
To adore the Conqueror, who now beholds
Cherub and seraph rolling in the flood
With scatter'd arms and ensigns, till anon
His swift pursuers from heaven-gates discern
The advantage, and descending, tread us down
Thus drooping, or with linked thunderbolts
Transfix us to the bottom of this gulf?
Awake, arise, or be for ever fall'n."
They heard, and were abashed, and up they sprung
Upon the wing; as when men wont to watch
On duty, sleeping found by whom they dread,
Rouse and bestir themselves ere well awake.
Nor did they not perceive the evil plight
In which they were, or the fierce pains not feel;
Yet to their general's voice they soon obey'd,
Innumerable. As when the potent rod
Of Amram's son, in Egypt's evil day,
Waved round the coast, up call'd a pitchy cloud
Of locusts, warping on the eastern wind,
That o'er the realm of impious Pharaoh hung
Like night, and darken'd all the land of Nile:
So numberless were those bad angels seen
Hovering on wing under the cope of hell.
'Twixt upper, nether, and surrounding fires;
Till at a signal given, the uplifted spear
Of their great sultan waving to direct
Their course, in even balance down they light

On the firm brimstone, and fill all the plain;
A multitude like which the populous north
Pour'd never from her frozen loins, to pass
Rhene or the Danaw, when her barbarous sons
Came like a deluge on the south, and spread
Beneath Gibraltar to the Libyan sands.
Forthwith from every squadron and each band
The heads and leaders thither haste where stood
Their great commander; godlike shapes and forms
Excelling human, princely dignities,
And powers that erst in heaven sat on thrones,
Though of their names in heavenly records now
Be no memorial, blotted out and rased
By their rebellion from the books of life.
Nor had they yet among the sons of Eve
Got them new names; till, wandering o'er the earth,
Through God's high sufferance for the trial of man,
By falsities and lies the greatest part
Of mankind they corrupted to forsake
God their Creator, and the invisible
Glory of him that made them to transform
Oft to the image of a brute adorn'd
With gay religions, full of pomp and gold,
And devils to adore for deities:
Then were they known to men by various names,
And various idols through the heathen world.
  Say, muse, their names then known, who first, who last
Roused from the slumber on that fiery couch,
At their great emperor's call, as next in worth
Came singly where he stood on the bare strand,
While the promiscuous crowd stood yet aloof.
The chief were those who from the pit of hell,
Roaming to seek their prey on earth, durst fix
Their seats long after next the seat of God,
Their altars by his altar, gods adored
Among the nations round, and durst abide

Jehovah thundering out of Sion, throned
Between the cherubim; yea, often placed
Within his sanctuary itself their shrines,
Abominations; and with cursed things
His holy rites and solemn feasts profaned,
And with their darkness durst affront his light.
First Moloch, horrid king, besmeared with blood
Of human sacrifice, and parents' tears;
Though for the noise of drums and timbrels loud
Their children's cries unheard, that passed through fire
To his grim idol. Him the Ammonite
Worshipp'd in Rabba and her watery plain,
In Argob and in Bashan, to the stream
Of utmost Arnon. Nor content with such
Audacious neighbourhood, the wisest heart
Of Solomon he led by fraud to build
His temple right against the temple of God
On that opprobrious hill; and made his grove
The pleasant valley of Hinnom, Tophet thence
And black Gehenna call'd, the type of hell.
Next Chemos, the obscene dread of Moab's sons,
From Aroer to Nebo, and the wild
Of southmost Abarim; in Hesebon
And Horonaim, Seon's realm, beyond
The flowery dale of Sibma clad with vines,
And Eleale to the asphaltic pool,
Peor his other name, when he enticed
Israel in Sittim, on their march from Nile,
To do him wanton rites, which cost them woe.
Yet thence his lustful orgies he enlarged
Even to that hill of scandal, by the grove
Of Moloch homicide; lust hard by hate;
Till good Josiah drove them thence to hell.
With these came they, who, from the bordering flood
Of old Euphrates to the brook that parts
Egypt from Syrian ground, had general names

Of Baalim and Ashtaroth; those male,
These feminine: for spirits, when they please,
Can either sex assume, or both; so soft
And uncompounded is their essence pure;
Not tied or manacled with joint or limb,
Nor founded on the brittle strength of bones,
Like cumbrous flesh; but, in what shape they choose,
Dilated or condensed, bright or obscure,
Can execute their aëry purposes,
And works of love or enmity fulfil.
For those the race of Israel oft forsook
Their living strength, and unfrequented left
His righteous altar, bowing lowly down
To bestial gods! for which their heads as low
Bow'd down in battle, sunk before the spear
Of despicable foes. With these in troop
Came Astoreth, whom the Phœnicians call'd
Astarte, queen of heaven, with crescent horns;
To whose bright image nightly by the moon
Sidonian virgins paid their vows and songs;
In Sion also not unsung, where stood
Her temple on the offensive mountain, built
By that uxorious king, whose heart, though large,
Beguiled by fair idolatresses, fell
To idols foul. Thammuz came next behind,
Whose annual wound in Lebanon allured
The Syrian damsels to lament his fate
In amorous ditties all a summer's day;
While smooth Adonis from his native rock
Ran purple to the sea, supposed with blood
Of Thammuz yearly wounded; the love-tale
Infected Sion's daughters with like heat;
Whose wanton passions in the sacred porch
Ezekiel saw when, by the vision led,
His eye survey'd the dark idolatries
Of alienated Judah. Next came one

Who mourn'd in earnest, when the captive ark
Maim'd his brute image, head and hands lopp'd off
In his own temple, on the grunsel edge,
Where he fell flat, and shamed his worshippers:
Dagon his name, sea-monster, upward man
And downward fish: yet had his temple high
Rear'd in Azotus, dreaded through the coast
Of Palestine, in Gath and Ascalon,
And Accaron and Gaza's frontier bounds.
Him followed Rimmon, whose delightful seat
Was fair Damascus, on the fertile banks
Of Abbana and Pharphar, lucid streams.
He also against the house of God was bold:
A leper once he lost, and gain'd a king,
Ahaz his sottish conqueror, whom he drew
God's altar to disparage and displace
For one of Syrian mode, whereon to burn
His odious offerings, and adore the gods
Whom he had vanquish'd. After these appear'd
A crew, who under names of old renown,
Osiris, Isis, Orus, and their train,
With monstrous shapes and sorceries abused
Fanatic Egypt and her priests, to seek
Their wandering gods disguised in brutish forms
Rather than human. Nor did Israel 'scape
The infection, when their borrow'd gold composed
The calf in Oreb; and the rebel king
Doubled that sin in Bethel and in Dan,
Likening his Maker to the grazed ox;
Jehovah, who in one night, when he pass'd
From Egypt marching, equall'd with one stroke
Both her firstborn and all her bleating gods.
Belial came last, than whom a spirit more lewd
Fell not from heaven, or more gross to love
Vice for itself: to him no temple stood,
Or altar smoked; yet who more oft than he

In temples and at altars, when the priest
Turns atheist, as did Eli's sons, who fill'd
With lust and violence the house of God:
In courts and palaces he also reigns,
And in luxurious cities, where the noise
Of riot ascends above their loftiest towers,
And injury and outrage; and when night
Darkens the streets, then wander forth the sons
Of Belial, flown with insolence and wine.
Witness the streets of Sodom, and that night
In Gibeah, when the hospitable door
Exposed a matron, to avoid worse rape.
These were the prime in order and in might:
The rest were long to tell, though far renown'd
The Ionian gods, of Javan's issue; held
Gods, yet confess'd later than heaven and earth,
Their boasted parents; Titan, heaven's firstborn,
With his enormous brood, and birthright seized
By younger Saturn; he from mightier Jove,
His own and Rhea's son, like measure found;
So Jove usurping reigned: these first in Crete
And Ida known, thence on the snowy top
Of cold Olympus, ruled the middle air
Their highest heaven; or on the Delphian cliff,
Or in Dodona, and through all the bounds
Of Doric land: or who with Saturn old
Fled over Adria to the Hesperian fields,
And o'er the Celtic roam'd the utmost isles.

All these and more came flocking: but with looks
Downcast and damp; yet such wherein appear'd
Obscure some glimpse of joy, to have found their chief
Not in despair, to have found themselves not lost
In loss itself: which on his countenance cast
Like doubtful hue: but he, his wonted pride
Soon recollecting, with high words, that bore
Semblance of worth, not substance, gently raised

Their fainting courage, and dispell'd their fears.
Then straight commands, that at the warlike sound
Of trumpets loud and clarions be uprear'd
His mighty standard: that proud honour claim'd
Azazel as his right, a cherub tall;
Who forthwith from the glittering staff unfurl'd
The imperial ensign; which, full high advanced,
Shone like a meteor streaming to the wind,
With gems and golden lustre rich emblazed,
Seraphic arms and trophies; all the while
Sonorous metal blowing martial sounds;
At which the universal host upsent
A shout, that tore hell's concave, and beyond
Frighted the reign of Chaos and old Night.
All in a moment through the gloom were seen
Ten thousand banners rise into the air
With orient colours waving: with them rose
A forest huge of spears; and thronging helms
Appear'd, and serried shields in thick array
Of depth immeasurable: anon they move
In perfect phalanx to the Dorian mood
Of flutes and soft recorders; such as raised
To height of noblest temper heroes old
Arming to battle; and instead of rage,
Deliberate valour breathed, firm and unmoved
With dread of death to flight or foul retreat:
Nor wanting power to mitigate and 'suage
With solemn touches troubled thoughts, and chase
Anguish, and doubt, and fear, and sorrow, and pain
From mortal or immortal minds. Thus they,
Breathing united force, with fixed thought,
Moved on in silence to soft pipes, that charm'd
Their painful steps o'er the burnt soil: and now
Advanced in view they stand; a horrid front
Of dreadful length and dazzling arms, in guise
Of warriors old with ordered spear and shield!

Awaiting what command their mighty chief
Had to impose: he through the armed files
Darts his experienced eye, and soon traverse
The whole battalion views, their order due,
Their visages and stature as of gods;
Their number last he sums. And now his heart
Distends with pride, and hardening in his strength
Glories: for never since created man
Met such embodied force, as named with these
Could merit more than that small infantry
Warr'd on by cranes: though all the giant brood
Of Phlegra with the heroic race were join'd
That fought at Thebes and Ilium, on each side
Mix'd with auxiliar gods; and what resounds
In fable or romance of Uther's son,
Begirt with British and Armoric knights;
And all who since, baptized or infidel,
Jousted in Aspramont or Montalban,
Damasco, or Marocco, or Trebisond,
Or whom Biserta sent from Afric shore,
When Charlemain with all his peerage fell
By Fontarabia. Thus far these beyond
Compare of mortal prowess, yet observed
Their dread commander: he, above the rest
In shape and gesture proudly eminent,
Stood like a tower; his form had yet not lost
All her original brightness; nor appear'd
Less than archangel ruin'd, and the excess
Of glory obscured; as when the sun, new risen,
Looks through the horizontal misty air
Shorn of his beams; or from behind the moon,
In dim eclipse, disastrous twilight sheds
On half the nations, and with fear of change
Perplexes monarchs. Darken'd so, yet shone
Above them all the archangel; but his face
Deep scars of thunder had intrench'd; and care

Sat on his faded cheek, but under brows
Of dauntless courage, and considerate pride
Waiting revenge; cruel his eye, but cast
Signs of remorse and passion, to behold
The fellows of his crime, the followers rather
(Far other once beheld in bliss), condemn'd
For ever now to have their lot in pain:
Millions of spirits for his fault amerced
Of heaven, and from eternál splendours flung
For his revolt, yet faithful how they stood,
Their glory wither'd: as when heaven's fire
Hath scathed the forest oaks, or mountain pines,
With singed top their stately growth, though bare,
Stands on the blasted heath. He now prepared
To speak; whereat their doubled ranks they bend
From wing to wing, and half enclose him round
With all his peers · attention held them mute.
Thrice he assay'd, and thrice, in spite of scorn,
Tears, such as angels weep, burst forth; at last
Words, interwove with sighs, found out their way.
"O myriads of immortal spirits! O powers
Matchless, but with the Almighty; and that strife
Was not inglorious, though the event was dire,
As this place testifies, and this dire change,
Hateful to utter! but what power of mind,
Foreseeing or presaging, from the depth
Of knowledge, past or present, could have fear'd,
How such united force of gods, how such
As stood like these, could ever know repulse?
For who can yet believe, though after loss,
That all these puissant legions, whose exile
Hath emptied heaven, shall fail to reascend
Self-raised, and repossess their native seat?
For me, be witness all the host of heaven,
If counsels different, or danger shunn'd
By me, have lost our hopes. But he who reigns

Monarch in heaven, till then as one secure
Sat on his throne upheld by old repute,
Consent or custom; and his regal state
Put forth at full, but still his strength conceal'd
Which tempted our attempt, and wrought our fall.
Henceforth his might we know, and know our own,
So as not either to provoke, or dread
New war, provoked; our better part remains
To work in close design, by fraud or guile,
What force effected not; that he no less
At length from us may find, who overcomes
By force hath overcome but half his foe.
Space may produce new worlds; whereof so rife
There went a fame in heaven that he ere long
Intended to create, and therein plant
A generation, whom his choice regard
Should favour, equal to the sons of heaven:
Thither, if but to pry, shall be perhaps
Our first eruption; thither or elsewhere;
For this infernal pit shall never hold
Celestial spirits in bondage, nor the abyss
Long under darkness cover. But these thoughts
Full counsel must mature: peace is despair'd;
For who can think submission? War, then, war,
Open or understood, must be resolved."
He spake; and, to confirm his words, outflew
Millions of flaming swords, drawn from the thighs
Of mighty cherubim; the sudden blaze
Far round illumined hell; highly they raged
Against the Highest, and fierce with grasped arms
Clash'd on their sounding shields the din of war,
Hurling defiance toward the vault of heaven.
There stood a hill not far, whose grisly top
Belch'd fire and rolling smoke; the rest entire
Shone with a glossy scurf; undoubted sign
That in his womb was hid metallic ore,

The work of sulphur. Thither, wing'd with speed,
A numerous brigade hasten'd: as when bands
Of pioneers, with spade and pickaxe arm'd,
Forerun the royal camp, to trench a field,
Or cast a rampart. Mammon led them on:
Mammon, the least erected spirit that fell
From heaven; for e'en in heaven his looks and thoughts
Were always downward bent, admiring more
The riches of heaven's pavement, trodden gold,
Than aught, divine or holy, else enjoy'd
In vision beatific: by him first
Men also, and by his suggestion taught,
Ransack'd the centre, and with impious hands
Rifled the bowels of their mother earth
For treasures, better hid. Soon had his crew
Open'd into the hill a spacious wound,
And digg'd out ribs of gold. Let none admire
That riches grow in hell; that soil may best
Deserve the precious bane. And here let those
Who boast in mortal things, and wondering tell
Of Babel, and the works of Memphian kings,
Learn how their greatest monuments of fame
And strength and art, are easily outdone
By spirits reprobate, and in an hour
What in an age they with incessant toil
And hands innumerable scarce perform.
Nigh on the plain, in many cells prepared,
That underneath had veins of liquid fire,
Sluiced from the lake, a second multitude
With wondrous art founded the massy ore,
Severing each kind, and scumm'd the bullion dross;
A third as soon had form'd within the ground
A various mould, and from the boiling cells,
By strange conveyance, fill'd each hollow nook:
As in an organ, from one blast of wind,
To many a row of pipes the sound-board breathes.

Anon, out of the earth a fabric huge
Rose like an exhalation, with the sound
Of dulcet symphonies and voices sweet,
Built like a temple, where pilasters round
Were set, and Doric pillars overlaid
With golden architrave; nor did there want
Cornice or frieze, with bossy sculptures graven:
The roof was fretted gold. Not Babylon,
Nor great Alcairo, such magnificence
Equall'd in all their glories, to enshrine
Belus or Serapis their gods, or seat
Their kings, when Egypt with Assyria strove
In wealth and luxury. The ascending pile
Stood fix'd her stately height; and straight the doors,
Opening their brazen folds, discover, wide
Within, her ample spaces o'er the smooth
And level pavement; from the arched roof,
Pendant by subtle magic, many a row
Of starry lamps and blazing cressets, fed
With naphtha and asphaltus, yielded light
As from a sky. The hasty multitude
Admiring enter'd; and the work some praise,
And some the architect: his hand was known
In heaven by many a tower'd structure high,
Where sceptred angels held their residence,
And sat as princes; whom the supreme King
Exalted to such power, and gave to rule,
Each in his hierarchy, the orders bright.
Nor was his name unheard or unadored
In ancient Greece, and in Ausonian land
Men call'd him Mulciber; and how he fell
From heaven they fabled, thrown by angry Jove
Sheer o'er the crystal battlements: from morn
To noon he fell, from noon to dewy eve,
A summer's day; and with the setting sun
Dropp'd from the zenith, like a falling star,

On Lemnos th' Ægean isle: thus they relate,
Erring; for he with his rebellious rout
Fell long before; nor aught avail'd him now
To have built in heaven high towers; nor did he 'scape
By all his engines, but was headlong sent
With his industrious crew to build in hell.
Meanwhile, the winged heralds, by command
Of sovereign power, with awful ceremony
And trumpets' sound, throughout the host proclaim
A solemn council, forthwith to be held
At Pandemonium, the high capital
Of Satan and his peers: their summons call'd
From every band and squared regiment
By place or choice the worthiest; they anon,
With hundreds and with thousands trooping came,
Attended; all access was thronged: the gates
And porches wide, but chief the spacious hall
(Though like a cover'd field, where champions bold
Wont ride in arm'd, and at the soldan's chair
Defied the best of Panim chivalry
To mortal combat, or career with lance),
Thick swarm'd both on the ground and in the air
Brush'd with the hiss of rustling wings. As bees
In spring-time, when the sun with Taurus rides,
Pour forth their populous youth about the hive
In clusters; they among fresh dews and flowers
Fly to and fro, or on the smoothed plank,
The suburb of their straw-built citadel,
New rubb'd with balm, expatiate and confer
Their state affairs: so thick the aëry crowd
Swarm'd and were straiten'd; till, the signal given,
Behold a wonder! They but now who seem'd
In bigness to surpass earth's giant sons,
Now less than smallest dwarfs, in narrow room
Throng numberless, like that Pygmean race
Beyond the Indian mount; or faëry elves,

Whose midnight revels, by a forest side
Or fountain, some belated peasant sees,
Or dreams he sees, while over head the moon
Sits arbitress, and nearer to the earth
Wheels her pale course; they on their mirth
Intent, with jocund music charm his ear:
At once with joy and fear his heart rebounds;
Thus incorporeal spirits to smallest forms
Reduced their shapes immense, and were at large,
Though without number still, amidst the hall
Of that infernal court. But far within,
And in their own dimensions, like themselves,
The great seraphic lords and cherubim
In close recess and secret conclave sat;
A thousand demigods on golden seats
Frequent and full. After short silence then,
And summons read, the great consult began.

NOTES.

l. 1. *Of man's first disobedience, and [of] the fruit—blissful seat.* Two adverbial adjuncts of the predicate *sing*. (*Gr.* 396, *note*.)

l. 2. *Whose—seat.* An adjective clause, qualifying *tree*. (*Gr.* 408.)

l. 4. *With loss of Eden.* An adverbial adjunct of *brought*.

Till—seat. A compound adverbial clause. Before *regain* insert *till one greater man.* These clauses are in a sort of *quasi-attributive* relation to the noun *loss* (see *Gr.* 362*); or they may be taken as adverbial clauses qualifying some such word as *lasting* (understood), which would agree with *loss*. With this passage compare 1 *Corinth.* xv. 21, 22.

l. 6. *That on*, &c. After *Horeb*, supply *didst inspire—chaos;* and before *of Sinai*, supply *that on the secret top*. We thus get two adjective clauses qualifying *muse*. The name *Sinai* properly belongs to the entire group of mountains which has given its name to the whole peninsula which it characterises in so remarkable a manner. In a narrower sense *Sinai* is the name of one lofty ridge of this group, the most northerly peak of which is Horeb; the most southerly (by a still narrower application of the name), Mount Sinai. There is little doubt that Horeb was the mountain on which the Law was actually delivered (see *Deut.* i. 6; iv. 18, &c.); but as this peak is a part of the Sinaitic ridge, the Law is also said to have been delivered on Sinai. (*Levit.* vii. 38.)

l. 8. *That Shepherd.* (See *Exod.* iii. 1; *Psalm* lxxvii. 20.)

l. 9. *In the beginning.* An adverbial adjunct of *rose*.

How the heavens—chaos. A substantive clause which may be taken either as the object of *taught* (in which case *the chosen seed* must be taken as in the adverbial relation to *taught;* see *Gr.* 373, 4), or as a substantive clause attached adverbially to *taught* (*Gr.* 407), in which case *seed* will be the object of *taught*.

l. 11. Before *Siloa's* insert *if*, and after *oracle of God* insert *delight thee more.* Two adverbial clauses of condition, qualifying *invoke* (*Gr.* 427). The fountain of Siloam is at the entrance of the valley of Tyropocon. Its waters have an irregular flow. They are first collected in a pool or reservoir, the overflow of which forms a small stream *Isaiah* viii. 6; *John* ix. 7.

l. 12. *Fast* = *close.*

l. 14. *That with—rhyme.* An adjective clause qualifying *song.* *To soar*, &c. A verb in the infinitive mood, in the objective relation to *intends.* (*Gr.* 366, 368.) *The Aonian Mount.* Parnassus. Aonia was anciently the name of that part of Bœotia which lay at the foot of Parnassus and Helicon.

l. 15. *While it pursues*, &c. An adverbial clause of time, qualifying the verb *soar.* (*Gr.* 416.)

l. 16. Before *rhyme* we must supply *while it pursues things unattempted yet in.* The conjunction *or* implies an *alternative*, so that the words or phrases which it connects cannot be attached *conjointly* to other words in the sentence. Hence *or* always involves two separate clauses (which must be obtained by filling up the ellipse when there is one) co-ordinate with each other, but which may be either principal or subordinate clauses as respects the entire sentence. (*Gr.* 443.)

l. 17. *That dost prefer—pure.* An adjective clause which may be attached indifferently to *thou* or to *spirit.* Consult 1 *Corinth.* iii. 16, 17; vi. 19.

l. 19. Read *Genesis* i. 2.

l. 20. *With mighty wings outspread.* An adverbial adjunct of *sat'st.*

l. 21. *Brooding* must be taken grammatically as qualifying the subject *thou* (understood); in sense it forms a kind of complement to the predicate *sat'st.* (*Gr.* 392.)

l. 22. *Pregnant.* Complement of the predicate *mad'st.* (*Gr.* 392, 396.)

What in me is dark. This is frequently called a substantive clause. It is really an adjective clause used substantively, that is, qualifying some demonstrative word understood; for *what*, being a relative pronoun (*Gr.* 153), properly introduces an adjective clause. (*Gr.* 408, 409).

l. 23. In full: *What is low, raise* [*thou*] *and* [*what is low*] *support* [*thou*].

l. 24. *That to the height—to men.* A compound adverbial clause, which must be repeated with each of the preceding predicates *instruct, illumine, raise*, and *support.* Between *and* and *justify* insert *that to the height of this great argument I may.*

l. 27. *For heaven*, &c. An adverbial clause of condition, attached to *say*.

l. 28. *Nor the deep tract of hell*, that is, *and the deep tract of hell hides nothing from thy view. What cause—besides. What* is here an interrogative word, and introduces a substantive clause (*Gr.* 403, 406), the object of *say*.

l. 29. *In that happy state.* An attributive adjunct of *parents.* (*Gr.* 362, 4.)

l. 30. *To fall off—to transgress.* Adverbial adjuncts of the predicate *moved.* (*Gr.* 190, 373, 2.)

l. 34. *He.* Complement of the predicate *was*, qualified by the complex adjective clause *whose guile—vain attempt.*

l. 36. *What time—vain attempt.* An adverbial clause of time attached to the predicate *deceived.*

l. 37. *With all his host—vain attempt*, is an adverbial adjunct of manner or circumstance attached to the verb *cast*, and consisting of a preposition followed by a noun, which has several complex attributive adjuncts.

l. 41. *If he opposed.* An adverbial clause qualifying *to have equalled* Before *with ambitious aim*, supply *by whose aid aspiring to set himself in glory above his peers he.*

l. 42. *Against the throne*, &c. An attributive adjunct of *aim.* (*Gr.* 362, 4.)

l. 47. *There to dwell*, &c. An adverbial adjunct of *hurled.* See *note* on *l.* 30.

l. 49. *Who durst*, &c. An adjective clause qualifying the object *him.*

l. 50. *Nine times the space*, &c. An adverbial adjunct of *lay.* (*Gr.* 373, 3.)

l. 53. *Though* [*he was*] *immortal.* An elliptical adverbial clause, qualifying the adjective or participle *confounded.*

l. 54. *For now*, &c. An adverbial clause attached to *reserved.*

l. 58. *With pride and hate.* An adverbial adjunct of *mixed.*

l. 59. *As angels ken*, i.e., *know* or *descry.* An adverbial clause coordinate with *as* which qualifies *far.* In full the clause is, *as angels ken far.* See *Gr.* 547, &c.

l. 62. *As one great furnace.* An elliptical adverbial clause attached to *flamed.* Supply after *furnace* the verb *flames.*

l. 63. *No light.* Supply *came* or *shone.*

l. 64. *To discover—unconsumed.* A complex adverbial adjunct of *served.* See *note* on *l.* 30.

l. 65. *Where peace—unconsumed.* An adjective clause qualifying *shades.* (*Gr.* 410.) It is compound and elliptical. Repeat *where* before *hope*, before *torture*, and before *a fiery deluge;* and after *unconsumed* supply *still urges.*

l. 67. *Without end.* An attributive adjunct of *torture.* (*Gr.* 362, 4.)

l. 71. With the verbs *ordained* and *set*, repeat the subject *eternal justice.*

l. 73. *Removed*, with its adverbial adjuncts *as far*, &c., qualifies the object *portion.*

As far. As qualifies *far*, and is itself explained by the elliptical adverbial clause, *as thrice* [*the distance*] *from the centre to the utmost pole* [*is far*], which is co-ordinate with *as.* (*Gr.* 547, &c.)

Phrases like *three times the distance, half the sum, a dozen men*, &c., are rather anomalous combinations, in which the two substantives are in a sort of apposition to each other.

l. 74. *From the centre* and *to the pole*, form attributive adjuncts of the noun *distance* understood. (*Gr.* 362, 4). Comp. *note* on *l.* 59.

The utmost pole, that is, of the universe, not of the *earth.* Milton treats the earth as the centre of the mundane system. See Book IX. 103, X. 671.

l. 75. After *fell*, supply *was this place. The place* is an adverbial adjunct of *unlike.* The preposition *to* may be supplied.

l. 81. After *Beelzebub*, supply *he soon discerns.*

l. 82. *And thence. And* is superfluous. The clause *to whom*, &c., is an adjective clause qualifying *one.* It goes on to *l.* 124.

l. 84. To establish a *grammatical* link of connection between this speech and the last sentence, we must understand some such phrase as *by saying*, so as to constitute an adverbial adjunct to the predicate, in apposition to *thus.* The connection of the clauses in the early part of the speech is extremely obscure. The best way, perhaps, is to consider the elliptical clauses, *O how fallen* [*thou art*], *how changed* [*thou art*] *from him—though bright*, as parenthetical, and the words *if he* as an elliptical repetition of the earlier clause *if thou beest he*, which will then form an adverbial clause of condition attached to the predicate *hath joined.* Unless this be done, *he* is ungrammatical, and should be altered to *him;* for if the conjunction *if* belongs to the same clause as *hath joined*, *he* must be the antecedent of *whom*, and ought to be the object of the verb. Moreover, it will be very difficult then to find out which is the main clause of the sentence. But by taking *if he* as a repetition of *if thou beest he*, *he* is in the right case, and *hath joined* is the predicate of the main clause. The clauses *O how fallen thou art, how changed thou art*, &c., may possibly be regarded as principal clauses, to the predicates of each of which the adverbial clause, *if thou beest he*, is attached. In that case *but* is superfluous. If the clauses are treated as parenthetical, there is no way of making sense of the *but* except by understanding some such clause as "*I think that thou art he*" before it. The elliptical clause *if he* will still qualify the verb *hath joined.*

l. 86. *Didst outshine.* This is not strictly grammatical. The relative *who* must agree with its antecedent *him* in person, and *him* cannot possibly be of the second person. (*Gr.* 468.)

l. 87. *Though* [*they were*] *bright.* An elliptical adverbial clause qualifying the predicate *didst outshine.*

Whom mutual league—once. An adjective clause qualifying an antecedent *him* understood, the object of *hath joined.* The subject of the relative clause is compound. (*Gr.* 386.)

l. 90. After *hath joined*, repeat *with me.*

The meaning is: "The distance between the *pit* and the *height* measures his superiority in strength." The construction is very crabbed. *What pit thou seest* is an adjective clause used substantively (*Gr.* 409) after *into.* The *what* before *height* is interrogative. The sentence cannot be treated by strict grammatical rules.

l. 94. After *for those*, insert the compound clause *do I repent—his throne. Nor* implies an alternative. We shall thus get four co-ordinate sentences:—1. *Not for those do I repent.* 2. *Not for those do I change—throne.* 3. *Not* [*for*] *what the potent—inflict do I repent.* 4. *Not* [*for*] *what the potent—inflict do I change—throne.*

l. 95. *What the—inflict.* An adjective clause used substantively. See *note* on *l.* 22. Supply *for* before *what. Else* should be taken as an attributive adjunct of *what.*

l. 97. *Though* [*I am changed*], &c. An elliptical adverbial clause qualifying the predicate *do change.*

l. 98. *From sense of injured merit.* An attributive adjunct of *disdain.* (*Gr.* 362, 4.)

l. 99. *That with—contend.* An adjective clause qualifying *disdain.*

l. 100. Repeat the relative *that* which is the subject (understood) of the clause, which is co-ordinate with the last.

l. 102. Three adjective clauses qualify *spirits.* 1. *That durst dislike*, &c. 2. *That—opposed*, &c. 3. *That shook his throne.*

l. 105. *What.* An elliptical interrogative clause. In full: *what care*

It or something of the sort, to the predicate of which the clause *though the field be lost* stands in the adverbial relation.

l. 106. *Is not lost* may be repeated with the several subjects *will, study, hate, courage, what else;* or these may be taken as forming a compound subject (*Gr.* 386) with the single predicate *are not lost.*

l. 108. *To submit* and *to yield* are attributive adjuncts of *courage.* (*Gr.* 362, 4.)

l. 110. *Wrath or might.* Make a separate sentence for each subject.

l. 111. The compound subject *to bow, to sue, and to deify,* &c., is repeated in the word *that* (*l.* 114), which may be left out in the analysis; or else *that* may be taken as the subject, having the infinitive moods in apposition to it.

l. 113. *Who from,* &c. An adjective clause qualifying the substantive pronoun *his.* (*Gr.* 141.)

l. 116. *Since by fate,* &c.; *since through,* &c. Adverbial clauses attached to the predicate of the preceding clause. There is no objection to taking them with the predicate of each of the two preceding clauses.

l. 122. *Irreconcilable* is an attributive adjunct of the subject *we.*

l. 123. After *and* repeat *who.*

l. 125, *Though* [*he was*] *in pain.* An elliptical adverbial clause, qualifying the predicate *spake.*

l. 128. See *note* on *l.* 84.

A vocative or nominative of appellation does not enter into the construction of a sentence.

l. 130. *And in dreadful deeds,* &c. Repeat the relative *that* as the subject of this clause.

l. 133. *Upheld* qualifies the noun *supremacy,* and is itself qualified by the adverbial phrases *by strength, by chance, by fate,* which are united together by the conjunctions *whether, or.*

l. 134. The object *events,* with all its adjuncts, must be repeated with each verb *see* and *rue.*

l. 136. *And all,* &c. Repeat the relative as the subject of the clause, and the auxiliary *hath.*

l. 137. *Low* is a complement of the predicate *laid.* (*Gr.* 395.)

l. 138. *Far* qualifies *hath laid,* and is itself qualified by the demonstrative adverb *as,* which in its turn is explained by the co-ordinate adverbial clause *as God's—can perish,* in which the word *far* is again understood, being qualified by the relative adverb *as* at the beginning of the clause. (On the analysis of all such clauses, see *Gr.* 548, 564.)

l. 139. *For the mind*, &c. This adverbial clause qualifies the predicate of a sentence understood, *I say as far*, or something of the sort.

l. 140. *Invincible* is the complement of the predicate *remains*. (*Gr*. 392.)

l. 141. The elliptical adverbial clauses *though all our glory* [*be*] *extinct*, and [*though*] *our happy state* [*be*] *here swallowed*, &c., may be attached to the predicate of each of the foregoing clauses, *remains* and *return*.

l. 143. After *but what* supply *are we to say*, or something equivalent. *Whom I now believe* [*to be*] *of almighty force*. The infinitive *to be*, with its subject *whom* forms a complex object of *believe*. (*Gr*. 397.) *Of almighty force* is an adverbial adjunct of *be*.

l. 144. *No less than such;* that is, in full, *no force less than such force is great*, where the adverbial clause of degree *than such*, &c., qualifies *less*. See *Gr*. 547, 559, 422.

l. 145. *As ours* [*was*]. An adjective clause co-ordinate with *such*. On the construction of such clauses see *Gr*. 412, and the note on 267, and 523.

l. 147. *Suffice* here means *satisfy*.

l. 148. *That we may—ire*. An adverbial clause of purpose, qualifying *have left*.

l. 149. [*That we may*] *do him mightier service*, &c. The whole of the preceding sentence *what if he our conqueror—support our pains* must be repeated with this adverbial clause, which is attached to its predicate *have left*.

As his thralls, &c. In full: *As his thralls by right of war do him mighty service*. An adverbial clause of manner, qualifying *may do*. *By right of war* is an attributive adjunct of *thralls*. (*Gr*. 362, 4.)

l. 150. *Whate'er* is the complement of the verb of incomplete predication *be*. (*Gr*. 392.) The clause is an adverbial clause of condition attached to the predicate *may do*. (*Gr*. 427.)

l. 151. *Here in the heart—deep*. These elliptical clauses form an expansion of the preceding clause. In full they are: *If his business be here in the heart of hell to work in fire, or if his business be to do his errands in the gloomy deep*. The whole sentence *what if he our conqueror—our pains, that we may do—of war*, should be repeated with each clause, since each of them qualifies the verb *may do*, and the conjunction *or* implies that we have alternatives, which can only be taken separately.

l. 154. Before *eternal being* supply *what can it then avail though yet we feel*.

l. 155. *To undergo eternal punishment.* This must be taken as an attributive adjunct (*Gr.* 362, 4) both of *strength* and of *being.*

l. 157. The whole of this speech forms the object of the verb *replied. Fallen cherub*, being a vocative, or nominative of appellation, does not enter into the construction of the clause.

To be weak, &c. In full: *To be weak doing is miserable; or to be weak suffering is miserable.* This is one of those instances in which the association of ideas conveyed by the language is definite enough, though the latter is not easily reducible within the limits of grammatical rules. How are the participles *doing* and *suffering* constructed? What do they agree with? The origin of the idiom is to be sought in the fact that a verb, even in the infinitive or substantive mood, never entirely loses its attributive character, and consequently presupposes some subject to which the attributive idea is attached; and the attributive participle is used on much the same principle as the attributive infinitive mood. The idiom may be reduced to a grammatical form by supplying *if we are*, or *when we are*, before *doing* and *suffering;* we then get adverbial clauses of condition or time qualifying the verb *is.*

l. 159. *To do*, &c. These are two substantive clauses in apposition to *this.* The conjunction *that* may be supplied at the beginning of each.

l. 160. After *ill* supply *will be.*

l. 161. *As being*, &c. An elliptical adverbial clause, qualifying the predicate (understood) *will be*, of the previous clause. The ellipse may be filled up thus:—*As* [*an act*] *being the contrary to his high will whom we resist* [*would be our sole delight*].

l. 162. *Whom we resist.* An adjective clause, qualifying the substantive pronoun *his.* See *note* on *l.* 113.

l. 163. *To bring forth good.* This may be taken either as the *object*, or as an *adverbial adjunct* to the verb *seek.* (*Gr.* 190, 368.)

l. 164. *To pervert evil*—compound complement of the verb of incomplete predication *be.* (*Gr.* 392.)

l. 166. *Which* is here *continuative* (*Gr.* 413), being equivalent to *and this.* It introduces a *principal* sentence. *As* does duty for a relative pronoun. (*Gr.* 412.) The words *as perhaps shall* must be repeated before *disturb.* We thus get two adjective clauses co-ordinate with *so*, just as they would be with *such*, if *in such a way* were substituted for *so.*

l. 167. *If I fail not.* That is, *if I am not mistaken.* An adverbial clause of condition qualifying *shall grieve.*

l. 177. *To bellow.* Object of the verb *ceases.* (*Gr.* 368.)

l. 178. *Let us slip.* It may be necessary to remind some that this phrase is not a *first* person plural of an imperative mood. *Let* is in the second person plural, having its subject *you* or *ye* understood, and *us* is the *object* of *let*. *Slip* is a verb in the infinitive mood, forming the complement of the verb of incomplete predication *let*, and itself having *occasion* for its object.

Whether scorn, &c. Expand this for analytical purposes, thus:—*Either if scorn yield it from our foe, or if satiate fury yield it from our foe.* This gives us two adverbial clauses of condition, attached to the predicate *let*.

l. 182. *Save what*, &c. *Save* (Fr. *sauf*) is in reality an adjective, qualifying the noun or the noun-sentence which follows it, and so forming a nominative absolute (see *Gr.* 283). Here *save* qualifies the antecedent (understood) of the adjective clause *what—dreadful.* (See *note* on *l.* 22.) The whole phrase *save what*, &c., forms an adverbial adjunct to the adjective *void*.

l. 183. *Let us tend.* See *note* on *l.* 178.

l. 184. *From off*, &c. As a preposition cannot govern anything but a substantive (*Gr.* 279), it is not easy to provide *from* with anything to govern. We must supply some such word as *the space* or *the region* between *from* and *off;* when the phrase *off the tossing*, &c., will become an attributive adjunct of the noun supplied. We must adopt a similar method with all such phrases. Thus *he appeared from under the table*, must be taken as *he appeared from the space, or position, under the table.*

l. 185, 187. *Rest—consult.* It will be better to treat these as elliptical, and read *let us rest, let us consult. Re-assembling* will then agree with the object *us* understood, and *our* will have a pronoun in the first person, to which it may relate.

l. 187. *How we may*, &c. A substantive clause, the object of *consult.*

l. 188. Fill up the ellipse thus:—*There let us consult how our own loss we may repair; there let us consult how we may overcome this dire calamity; there let us consult what reinforcement we may gain from hope; if we may not gain reinforcement from hope, there let us consult what resolution we may gain from despair.*

l. 190. *What*, being interrogative, introduces a *substantive* clause. (*Gr.* 406.)

l. 192. After *thus Satan*, supply *spoke.*

l. 193. *With head*, &c. An adverbial adjunct of *spoke.*

l. 194. The adverb *besides* qualifies the verb *lay.*

l. 196. *In bulk.* An adverbial adjunct of *huge.*

l. 197. *As whom,* &c. Elliptical adverbial clause, co-ordinate with *as* before *huge.* In full: *as [they] whom the fables name of monstrous size [were huge].* The construction of the whole of this passage is very obscure. Perhaps the best way to take it is to consider the phrase *of monstrous size* as an attributive adjunct of *they* understood; and the word *Titanian* (which is *adjective* in its form) as the complement of the predicate *name,* as though the sentence ran thus: *as they of monstrous size that warred on Jove, whom the fables name Titanian. Earth-born* must then be treated like *Titanian.* Those acquainted with classical mythology will not need to be told that the Titans and the Giants or Earth-born are not the same, though both warred with Zeus, or Jupiter. Briareos, or Ægæon, is by some ancient writers classed among the Gigantes. All the mythological personages here mentioned were the offspring of Earth (Ge or Gæa). According to the common version, Briareos and his two brothers, Gyges and Cottus, were hundred-handed monsters—the offspring of Uranus and Gæa. The Titans were another group of the offspring of Uranus and Gæa. The Titans, headed by Cronus, deposed Uranus; and Zeus, the son of Cronus, in his turn, with the aid of Briareos and his two brothers, deposed Cronus and the Titans, and imprisoned them in Tartarus, placing the Hundred-handed to guard them. The attempt of the Gigantes to overthrow Zeus, or Jupiter, and the similar attempt of Typhon or Typhoeus, are separate incidents in the mythology. Virgil, however, amongst others, reckons Briareos among the Gigantes. The use of the conjunction *or* obliges us to amplify this passage for analysis as follows: 1. *His other parts—Titanian, that warred on Jove.* 2. The same repeated, with the substitution of *Earth-born* for *Titanian.* 3. *His other parts—huge, as [he] of monstrous size [was huge], whom the fables name Briareos.* 4. The same as the last, with the substitution of *Typhon, whom the den—held* for *Briareos.* 5. *His other parts—huge as that sea-beast,* &c.

l. 200. *By ancient Tarsus.* An attributive adjunct of *den.*

l. 202. *Hugest.* Complement of the predicate *created.* (*Gr.* 395.)

That swim the ocean stream. An adjective clause qualifying *works.* The cosmology of Homer represented the earth as a circular flat disc, round the outer edge of which ran a river or stream called Oceanus. Heaven (*Uranus*) was a hemispherical vault above the flat earth; and Tartarus a corresponding inverted vault beneath it.

l. 203. *Him,* object of *deeming.*

l. 205. *Island,* complement of the participle *deeming.* (*Gr.* 395.)

l. 206. *In his scaly rind.* Adverbial adjunct of *fixed.*

l. 208. Insert *while* before *wished.* The clauses, *as seamen tell, while night invests the sea,* and *while wished morn delays,* are adverbial clauses attached to the predicate *moors.*

l. 210. *Chained* may be taken as the complement of *lay.* In analysis *nor ever* may be treated as equivalent to *and never.*

l. 211. First leave out *or heaved his head,* and take all that remains from *nor ever thence* to *vengeance poured,* as one compound sentence. Next repeat this sentence, substituting *had raised his head* for *had risen.*

There are certain constructions in which *but* is a preposition. (*Gr.* 282, *note.*) It is so used here, governing the substantive clause *that the will—vengeance poured,* the preposition and substantive clause together forming an adverbial adjunct, attached to the predicates *had risen* and *had heaved.* (*Gr.* 403.)

l. 214. *That with,* &c. An adverbial clause of purpose, qualifying *left.* (On the adverbial force of the so-called conjunction *that* in such clauses, see *Gr.* 528.)

l. 216. Insert *that* and the subject *he* in this sentence, which is constructed like the last.

l. 217. *How all—poured,* &c. A substantive clause (*Gr.* 403), the object of *see.*

l. 217. Respecting this use of *but,* see *Gr.* 505.

To bring forth, &c. An adverbial adjunct of *served.* (*Gr.* 190.)

l. 219. *But* is here a co-ordinative conjunction (*Gr.* 287, 288), and unites *confusion, wrath, and vengeance* to the preceding objects of *bring,* namely, *goodness, grace,* and *mercy.*

On himself is an adverbial adjunct of *poured.*

l. 221. *Upright.* Complement of the predicate *rears.* (*Gr.* 395.)

l. 221. *From off.* See *note* on *l.* 184.

l. 223. Before *rolled,* insert *on each hand the flames.*

l. 227. *Till—lights.* An adverbial clause of time, attached to *steers.*

l. 228. *If it were,* &c. An adverbial clause of condition, qualifying the predicate of a sentence which must be supplied, *I say land,* or something of that kind.

That ever burned—fire. An adjective clause qualifying *it.* After *solid* insert *fire,* and after *lake* insert *burned.*

l. 230. *Such.* Complement of the predicate *appeared.* (*Gr.* 392.) Before *such* insert *that* or *which.* The passage from *and [that] such appeared* to *smoke,* is another adjective clause attached to *it.*

After *as* insert *land appears.* From *as when* (*l.* 230) to *smoke* (*l.* 237) is a compound adverbial clause, co-ordinate with the adjective *such* (*l.* 230). From *when* to *smoke* makes a subordinate adverbial clause of time, qualifying *appears* understood. It must be sub-divided into two others. First leave out *or the shattered side of thundering Ætna;* next, in the sentence so obtained, for *from Pelorus,* substitute *from the shattered side of thundering Ætna.* Both the adverbial clauses thus formed qualify *appears.*

l. 236. Before *leave* repeat *whose combustible—fury.*

l. 239. *Both glorying,* &c. A nominative absolute, forming an adverbial adjunct of *followed.*

l. 240. *As gods.* That is, *as gods* [*would have escaped the Stygian flood*]. This adverbial clause, and the two succeeding adverbial phrases, are attached to the infinitive mood *to have escaped.*

l. 242. After *region, soil,* and *clime,* supply the adjective clause *that we must change for heaven.* Before *this the soil* put in *is;* before *the clime* put in *is this;* before *this the seat* put in *is;* and before *this mournful gloom* supply *must we change.* The whole passage, down to *l.* 270, is the object of the verb *said.*

l. 245. *Since he,* &c. A compound adverbial clause attached to the predicate *he.* The clause consists of two co-ordinate clauses. 1. *Since he who now is sovran can dispose what shall be right.* 2. *Since he—sovran can bid what—right.*

l. 247. *What shall be right.* See *note* on *l.* 22.

l. 247. *Farthest.* That is, *the place farthest. From him whom,* &c., is an adverbial adjunct of *him.*

l. 248. Before *force* repeat *whom. Supreme* is the complement of *made.* (*Gr.* 396.)

l. 249. *Farewell.* That is, *fare ye well.* (Compare *Gr.* 532.)

Happy fields. Vocatives are of the nature of interjections, and do not enter into the construction of the sentences in which they are placed.

l. 252. *One.* In apposition to, and therefore an attributive adjunct of *possessor.*

l. 254. *And in itself,* &c. Expand thus: [*the mind*] *in itself can make a heaven of hell;* [*the mind in itself can make*] *a hell of heaven.*

l. 255. *Can make a heaven of hell.* Here *heaven* is the direct object of *make, of hell* being an adverbial adjunct of *make.* If we were to say *can make hell a heaven,* then *hell* would be the object of the verb, and *heaven* would be the complement of the predicate. (Compare *l.* 248.)

l. 256. In full: *what matter* [*is it*] *where* [*I be*], *if I be still the same, and* [*if*] *what I should be* [*be*] *all but less than he—greater.* Observe that in a question such as *what matter is it*, *it* is the subject, and *what matter* is the complement of the verb of incomplete predication *is*. The construction of interrogative clauses is always to be tested by that of corresponding assertive clauses. *What matter is it?* answers to *it is this matter*, or *it is no matter*. The clause *where I be* is an adjective clause qualifying the subject *it*, just as in such a sentence as *it was John who told me*, the construction is: *It* (i.e., *the person*) *who told me was John*. (*Gr.* 511, 513).

l. 257. *What I should be.* (See *note* on *l.* 22.)

l. 257. *Than he*, &c. In full, *than he whom thunder has made greater is great*. An adverbial clause, qualifying *less*. (*Gr.* 548—558.) *But* is here a preposition (see *l.* 211, *note*), and the whole phrase *but less—greater*, forms an adverbial adjunct to *all*.

l. 260. *Envy* in Milton commonly has the sense of the Latin *invidia* and *invidere*, implying *grudging*.

l. 262. Before *in hell* supply *one reign*, or something equivalent.

l. 263. In full. *To reign in hell* [*is*] *better than to serve in heaven* [*is good*]. The adverbial clause *than to serve*, &c., qualifies *better*, showing the degree of *better* that is meant.

l. 266. *Lie* is the complement of the verb of incomplete predication *let*, and *astonished* is the complement of *lie*.

l. 267. *And call.* In full: *and wherefore call we.*

To share—mansion. An adverbial phrase attached to *call*. (*Gr.* 190, 373, 2.)

l. 268. After *or* supply *wherefore call we them not*.

l. 269. *What may—heaven.* A substantive clause. *What* is interrogative. (*Gr.* 403. Compare *note* on *l.* 22.) *Be regained* is the complement of the verb of incomplete predication *may*.

l. 270. Before *what* supply *wherefore call we them not once more with rallied arms to try*. After *more* insert *may be*.

l. 272. See *note* on *l.* 83, 84.

l. 273. *But* is here a preposition. *But the omnipotent* forms an adverbial phrase (*Gr.* 373, 2) qualifying *none*.

l. 274. *If once.* Some writers very absurdly affect the omission of *if* and *when* in phrases of this kind. The blunder is frequent in modern periodical writing.

l. 274. *Pledge* with its complicated adjuncts, and *signal*, are in apposition to *voice*.

l. 276. Repeat *heard* before *on*. The adverbial clause *when it raged*, will then qualify the participle so supplied.

l. 277. *In all assaults* forms an attributive adjunct to *signal.* (*Gr.* 362, 4.)

l. 279. Before [*they will soon*] *revive*, repeat the whole sentence *if once—signal;* and the clause *though now—amazed*, must be taken with each of the sentences so formed, qualifying the predicates *will resume* and *will revive.*

l. 280. *Grovelling* and *prostrate* are complements of the predicate *lie.*

l. 281. After *erewhile* supply *lay.*

l. 282. In full: *it was no wonder that we, fallen such a pernicious height, lay astounded and amazed.* The clause *that we*, &c., is a substantive clause in apposition to *it.* (*Gr.* 511.)

Such a height forms an adverbial phrase qualifying *fallen.* (*Gr.* 373, 3.)

l. 284. *His shield cast:* a nominative absolute, forming an adverbial adjunct of *was moving.* (*Gr.* 373, 5.)

l. 285. [*Of*] *ethereal temper:* an attributive adjunct of *shield.* (*Gr.* 362, 4.)

l. 287. The phrase [*to*] *the moon* is adverbial in its force, and qualifies *like*, which agrees with the subject *circumference.*

l. 288. *The Tuscan artist.* Galileo.

l. 290. Before *in Valdarno* we must repeat *whose orb—at evening.* The adverbial phrase *to descry*, &c. (*Gr.* 190), belongs to both sentences, and must therefore be inserted after *Fesole*, as well as after *Valdarno.* It must, however, be separated into three separate phrases:—1. *To descry new lands in her spotty globe.* 2. *To descry new rivers*, &c. 3. *To descry new mountains*, &c.

l. 292. Take *he walked with* before *his spear.*

To equal—wand. A complex adjective phrase qualifying *spear.* *To equal which* is an adverbial phrase attached to *were.*

l. 293. *To be the mast*, &c. An adverbial phrase qualifying *hewn.*

l. 297. The word *clime* (clima) in ancient writers, means much the same as *zone*, and is loosely applied both to the terrestrial zones and to analogous divisions of the (supposed) vault of heaven, as Virgil says (Georg. I. 233): *Quinque tenent cœlum zonæ.* It is obvious that Milton has this latter application of the word in mind.

l. 299. *Nathless.* That is, *na* (or *not*) *the less.*

l. 300. Before *called* supply *till he.* This clause and the last are adverbial clauses of time, qualifying *endured.*

l. 301. The compound clause *who lay—chariot-wheels*, is an adjective clause qualifying *legions.*

l. 302. *Thick*, &c., had better be taken as an attributive adjunct of *who.*

As autumnal leaves that—imbower [*are thick*]. An adverbial clause of degree (*Gr.* 421) attached to *thick.* The adverb *as* at the beginning of the clause qualifies *thick*, understood.

l. 303. *Where—imbower.* An adjective clause qualifying Vallombrosa. (*Gr.* 410.)

l. 304. Before *scattered* introduce *as*, and after *afloat* supply *is thick.* This clause (which goes on to *l.* 311), like the last, qualifies *thick* in *l.* 302. The clause from *when* to *chariot-wheels* is an adverbial clause of time attached to *is*, supplied in *l.* 304.

l. 306. *The Red Sea coast, whose*, &c. This is a harsh construction, as the combination of words *Red Sea coast* forms in fact a single compound noun, whereas *whose* is intended to refer to *Red Sea* only. For analytical purposes it may be altered to *the coast of the Red Sea.* The adjective clause, *whose waves*, &c., goes on to the word *chariot-wheels.*

l. 307. To give the name Busiris to the Pharaoh of the Exodus is a mere poetic licence. The Busiris of the Greek writers was a merely mythical personage. No king of that name occurs even in the dynasties of Manetho.

l. 308. *While—chariot-wheels.* A compound adverbial sentence qualifying *o'erthrew.*

l. 309. *Who beheld*, &c. An adjective clause qualifying the object *sojourners.*

l. 311. Take *bestrown, abject*, and *lost* as complements of *lay.*

l. 313. *Under amazement*, &c. An adverbial adjunct of *lay.*

l. 314. *That all—resounded.* An adverbial clause co-ordinate with *so.* (*Gr.* 518.)

l. 317. *If such*, &c. An adverbial clause of condition qualifying the adjective *lost.*

l. 317. *As this* [*astonishment is*]. An adjective clause co-ordinate with *such.* See *Gr.* 412.

l. 318. *Or have ye*, &c. There is no grammatical connection between this sentence and the preceding words, which merely form a complex vocative. *Or* must either be left out, or treated as equivalent to *whether.*

l. 319. *After the toil of battle.* An adverbial adjunct of *repose.*

l. 320. *Virtue* = virtus (*valour*). *For the ease—heaven.* An adverbial adjunct of *have chosen.* Before *you find* supply *which.*

l. 321. *To slumber here*, &c. An attributive adjunct of *ease.* (*Gr.*

362, 4.) *As* [*ye slumbered*] *in the vales of heaven* is an adverbial clause qualifying *to slumber*.

l. 325. *With arms and ensigns.* An adverbial adjunct of the participle *rolling*.

Till anon—gulf. A compound adverbial clause of time qualifying *rolling*. It might almost equally well be attached to the verb *beholds*. In full: *till anon—advantage, and* [*till his swift pursuers*] *descending—drooping, or* [*till his swift pursuers*]*—gulf*.

l. 332. Before *when* insert *men spring up*.

The old meaning of *watch* is *keep awake*.

l. 333. Supply *him* before *whom*.

l. 334. First leave out *and bestir*, and then repeat the whole sentence *up they sprang—awake*, substituting *bestir* for *rouse*. After *ere* put in *they are*. We thus get an adverbial clause of time qualifying *rouse* and *bestir*.

l. 335. [*And*] *they did not not perceive*, &c. Take the first *not* with *did*, and the second with its complement *perceive*.

l. 336. In analysis, for *or* substitute [*and*] *they did not*.

l. 337. *To*, &c. The old-fashioned construction. See *Rom.* vi. 16. *His servants ye are to whom ye obey.*

l. 338. After *as* put in *the locusts were numberless:* to the verb *were*, thus supplied, the compound adverbial clause *when—Nile* is attached. The whole adverbial sentence is co-ordinate with *so* in *l.* 344.

l. 339. *Amram's son.* Moses. (See *Exodus* vi. 20.)

l. 340. *Waved*, a participle agreeing with *wand*.

l. 341. To *warp* is to move forward with a zigzag or unsteady motion.

l. 343. *Like night.* (See note on *l.* 287.) Before *darkened* repeat *that*.

l. 344. Take *numberless* as an attributive adjunct of *angels*, and *hovering* as the complement (*Gr.* 392, 323) of the verb *were seen*.

l. 347. *Till at—brimstone.* An adverbial clause, qualifying *were seen*. *The uplifted spear waving*, is a nominative absolute, forming an adverbial adjunct to *light*. (*Gr.* 373, 5.)

l. 350. Before *All* repeat *till at a—their course, they.* Another adverbial clause co-ordinate with the last.

l. 351. *Multitude*, with its adjuncts, is in apposition to *they*, and must be taken in *each* of the preceding adverbial clauses.

l. 351. *Like which—sands.* An adjective clause qualifying *multitude*.

l. 352. After *loins* supply *a multitude;* the adjective *like* will then agree with this noun; *which* being in the adverbial relation to *like*. (See *note* on *l.* 287.)

l. 353. First leave out *or the Danaw*, and take all that remains as one sentence; then repeat the whole, substituting *the Danaw* for *Rhene*. *Rhene* is an affected imitation of the Latin form *Rhenus*, while *Danaw* is a rather clumsy approximation to the German *Donau*.

l. 354. Before *spread* repeat *when her barbarous sons*. Both these adverbial clauses of time qualify *poured*.

l. 357. *Where stood*, &c. This is an adjective clause, defining the idea of place involved in the word *thither*. For analysis, *to that place* had better be substituted for *thither* (*Gr.* 410). The nouns *shapes*, *forms*, *dignities*, and *powers*, are in apposition to *heads* and *leaders*.

l. 360. *Erst* is the superlative (Germ. *erst*), answering to the comparative *ere* (Germ. *eher*).

l. 361. *Though—life*. An adverbial clause of *condition*, qualifying *sat*. *Blotted* and *rased* must be taken to agree with *names*. The only way of making the participles refer to *memorial* (which is in some respects the most natural), would be to supply the words *the memorial being* before *blotted*. We should then get a nominative absolute forming an adverbial adjunct to *be*. (*Gr.* 373, 5.)

l. 365. *Them* is in the adverbial relation to *got*. (*Gr.* 373, 4.)

Till—deities. A compound adverbial clause of time, qualifying the predicate *got*.

l. 368. *To forsake*, &c.; *to transform*, &c.; and *to adore*, &c., form adverbial adjuncts of *corrupted*. (*Gr.* 190, 373, 2.)

l. 372. *Religions* = Lat. *religiones* (religious ceremonies).

l. 376. *Say—aloof*. Make two co-ordinate sentences of this, by first leaving out *who last*, and then substituting *who last* for *who first*. The construction is: *Say the then known names of those who*, &c. *Their* is a *substantive* pronoun in the possessive case. (*Gr.* 141).

l. 378. *As next in worth*. An elliptical adverbial clause, qualifying *came*. In full: *As* [*potentates*] *next in worth* [*would come*].

l. 381. *From the pit of hell*. An adverbial adjunct of *roaming*.

l. 382. *Fix*, complement of the verb of incomplete predication *durst*.

l. 383. [*To*] *the seat of God* is in the adverbial relation to the adjective *next*, which is the complement of the verb *fix*.

l. 384. Repeat *who from the pit of hell roaming to seek their prey on earth durst fix*, before *their altar;* and *who from the pit—on earth* before *durst abide*, before *often placed* (*l.* 387), before *with cursed things* (*l.* 389), and before *with their darkness* (*l.* 391). We then get a series of adjective clauses qualifying *these*. *Gods* (*l.* 384) is in apposition to *who*.

l. 387. *Yea* is in reality an interjection.

l. 392. Supply the predicate *came* in this sentence.

l. 393. Put in *with* before *parents'*.

l. 394. *Though*, &c. This adverbial clause must be attached to *besmeared*. The force of the conjunction *though* is not very evident. Supply *were* before *unheard*. (Compare *Levit*. xviii. 21; *Jer*. vii. 31; xxxii. 35.)

l. 396. *Him the Ammonite worshipped*. See 1 *Kings* xi. 5, 7. It appears from these passages that Miloom was another name for Moloch or Molech.

l. 397. *Rabba*. See 2 *Samuel* xii. 26, 27.

l. 398. *Argob*. See *Numbers* xxi. 13—15; *Deut*. iii. 10—16.

l. 399. Take *nor* as equivalent to *and not*.

l. 401. *To build*, &c. An adverbial adjunct of *led*. (*Gr*. 190, 373, 2.)

l. 403. *That opprobrious hill*. A portion of the Mount of Olives, which lay *before*, *i.e.*, to the east of Jerusalem.

Grove is the complement of the predicate *made*, the object of which is *valley*.

l. 404. The origin of the name Tophet is disputed. One derivation is from Toph, *a drum* (see *l.* 394). The valley of Hinnom, or Gehenna, was on the south-east of Jerusalem.

l. 406. Supply the predicate *came*.

l. 407. *From Aroer to—Abarim*. An attributive adjunct of *dread*. The construction is very crabbed. The passage means, *Chemos, who was dreaded (or worshipped) by Moab's sons from Aroer*, &c.

l. 407. *Aroer*. There were four towns of this name. The one here meant was situated on the river Arnon. *Abarim* was a ridge of mountains to the east of the Dead Sea. It appears that *Nebo* was the name of one mountain in the ridge, and *Pisgah* the name of the highest peak of that mountain. (*Deut*. xxxii. 49; xxxiv. 1.)

l. 408. *Hesebon* or *Heshbon*. See *Numbers* xxi. 26.

l. 410. Compare *Isaiah* xvi. 8, 9.

l. 411. *Asphaltic pool*. Josephus calls the Dead Sea the *Limne Asphaltites*. The bed of the lake contains large quantities of bitumen, lumps of which are frequently detached, and rise to the surface. From the excessive saltness of its waters, it is called (*Genesis* xiv. 3) the *Salt Sea*. At the southern end the lake appears to have broken through its original boundary, and submerged the cities of the plain (Sodom, Gomorrah, &c.)

l. 412. After *Peor*, supply *being* or *was*, either of which will be qualified by the adverbial clause *when he enticed—woe.*

l. 416. *By the grove.* An attributive adjunct of *hill.*

l. 417. After *lust*, supply *being*. The adverbial phrase thus formed (see *Gr.* 373, 5) may be attached to *enlarged.*

l. 418. *Till*, &c. An adverbial clause qualifying *enlarged.*

l. 419. *The bordering flood.* See *Genesis* xv. 18.

l. 420. *The brook.* Frequently called, in our version, "The *river* of Egypt," an epithet which ought properly to be applied only to the Nile. This confusion of names does not exist in the original. The brook meant is now called the Wady-el-Arish, running past the town of El-Arish, which is called by Greek writers Rhinocorura. The phrases *from the bordering Euphrates*, and *to the brook—ground*, form adverbial adjuncts of *had.*

l. 422. *Baälim* and *Ashtaroth* are plurals. Baal and Ashtoreth are singular. After *those* and *these* supply *being*. We thus get two nominatives absolute, forming adverbial adjuncts, qualifying *had*, and denoting an *attendant circumstance.* The participle *being*, in each, is qualified by the compound adverbial clause *for spirits—or both*, which is separable into two co-ordinate clauses. 1. *For spirits, when they please, can either sex assume.* 2. *For spirits, when they please, can both sexes assume.*

l. 426. We get here five attributive adjuncts of *essence.* 1. *Not tied with joint.* 2. *Not manacled with joint.* 3. *Not tied with limb.* 4. *Not manacled with limb.* 5. *Not founded on the brittle strength of bones.* The participle in each of these is qualified by the adverbial phrase *like cumbrous flesh*, which must be repeated in each.

l. 428. *In what shape they choose.* An adverbial adjunct, consisting of a preposition governing an adjective clause used substantively, attached to each of the infinitives *execute*, and *fulfil.*

l. 429. We have in this sentence three co-ordinate principal clauses. 1. *In what shape they choose they can execute their aery purposes.* 2. *In what shape they choose they can fulfil works of love.* 3. *In what shape they choose they can fulfil works of enmity.* If the adjectives in *l.* 429 qualify *they*, *all* the above clauses must be repeated with *each* of these adjectives introduced into it, so that we shall get twelve sentences altogether. If *dilated*, &c., refer to *shape*, each of these adjectives must be expanded into an adverbial clause: [*if they choose a*] *dilated* [*shape*], &c., then *all* the three principal clauses must be repeated with *each* of these adverbial clauses attached to the predicates, giving us twelve in all, as before.

l. 433. Before *unfrequented*, repeat *for these the race of Israel oft.*

l. 435. *For which.* Take these words as equivalent to *and for this. Which* does not refer to any particular word. Take *bowed* as the predicate, and *sunk* as an attributive adjunct of *heads. As* is used as a simple adverb, in the sense of *equally.*

l. 439. *Queen—horns.* Attributive adjunct of *Ashtoreth.*

l. 442. *Where stood—idols foul.* An adjective clause, qualifying *Sion.* (Compare line 403, and 1 *Kings* xi. 5.)

l. 444. *Though* [*it was*] *large.* An adverbial clause attached to *fell.*

The idolatry of the Syrians, Phœnicians, and other Eastern nations embodied one feature, which, under various modifications, was essentially the same,—that is, the worship of the fecundating and productive powers of nature, personified in a male and a female divinity, called Baal (or Bel) and Ashtoreth (or Astarte); the former being commonly symbolized by, or identified with, the sun, the latter with the earth, or (more commonly) the moon. There was naturally a good deal of confusion between the sun and the moon in the above-mentioned symbolical aspect, and the sun and the moon simply as heavenly bodies. Hence we find *all the host of heaven* associated with Baal and Ashtoreth (2 *Kings* xxiii. 4, where the word rendered *grove* is a name for Ashtoreth, or at least for her image.) In Babylon the astrological aspect of the religion prevailed; and sometimes Baal and Ashtoreth were identified with the planets Jupiter and Venus. The Greeks naturally found a great deal of resemblance between Astarte and their own Aphrodite. As the supreme female divinity, she was also confounded with Hera, or Juno. As identified with the moon, she sometimes bears the name Diana. The Diana of the Ephesians was identical with Ashtoreth. Among the Tyrians Baal was called Melkarth. whom the Greeks spoke of as the Tyrian Hercules.

l. 446. Thammuz was the same as the mythological personage whom the Greeks called Adonis. He was represented as a beautiful youth, beloved by Aphrodite, who was killed by a boar, but was allowed by Zeus to spend part of every year with his beloved Aphrodite in the upper world. The Grecian myth was of Syrian or Phœnician origin. Thammuz appears to have been a personification of the tender verdure of spring wounded and destroyed by the parching heats of summer, and during the winter buried, as it were, in the lower world, but re-appearing again with the return of spring. A little Syrian river rising in Lebanon was called Adonis. Its waters are in fact tinged red after heavy rains by the soil through which it flows. The connection between the name of the youth and that of the river is not clearly made out.

l. 451. *Purple* is the complement of *ran*. *Supposed* must be amplified into an adverbial clause (*as it was supposed*), which, like the adverbial phrase *with blood—wounded*, is attached to the adjective *purple*.

l. 455. See *Ezekiel* viii. 13.

l. 459. *Head and hands lopped off*. A nominative absolute, forming an adverbial adjunct of *maimed*.

l. 460. *Grunsel=groundsill*, *i.e.*, threshold.

l. 461. Before *shamed* repeat *where he*. See 1 *Sam*. v. 4.

l. 462. A very crabbed construction. Perhaps *Dagon* [*being*] *his name* had better be taken as a nominative absolute, forming an adverbial adjunct (*Gr*. 373, 5) to *came*; and *sea-monster*, *man*, and *fish*, as attributive adjuncts of *one*. *Man* and *fish*, being in fact *adjectives* in force, are qualified by adverbs.

l. 463. After *yet* supply *he*.

l. 464. Azotus is the same as Ashdod.

Dreaded agrees with *he* understood (*l.* 463).

l. 465. See 1 *Samuel* vi. 17. *Gen*. x. 19.

l. 470. See 2 *Kings* v.

l. 472. *Ahaz* is in apposition to *king* and *conqueror*, and the adjective clause *whom he drew—vanquished* is in the attributive relation to *Ahaz*.

l. 474. The phrases *whereon to burn*, &c., and [*whereon to*] *adore*, &c., are attributive adjuncts of *altar* (understood) in "for one *altar*."

l. 477. *Under names*, &c. An adverbial adjunct of *abused*.

l. 480. *To seek—forms*. An adverbial adjunct of *abused*. The adverb *rather* qualifies *seek*, and is itself qualified and defined by the adverbial clause *than* [*they sought their wandering gods soon*] *in human* [*forms*]. (See *Gr*. 547, 555, 556.) Osiris and Isis were to the Egyptians much the same as Baal and Ashtoreth to the Syrian nations.

l. 481. *Brutish forms*. The bull Apis was usually represented as a symbol or incarnation of Osiris. Anubis was represented as a dog, or with a dog's head; Horus with the head of a hawk; Ammon as a ram, or with the head of a ram; Mendes as a goat. Numerous animals, also, as the dog, cat, goat, crocodile, ichneumon, monkey, ibis, hawk, &c., were objects of religious worship.

l. 482. *Nor did Israel escape*, i.e., *And Israel did not escape*, &c.

The worship of the golden calf was of course borrowed from that of the bull Apis.

l. 484. *The rebel king.* Jeroboam. See 1 *Kings* xii.

l. 488. *Equalled.* That is, *levelled, laid low.*

l. 490. *Than whom a spirit—heaven,* and [*than whom a spirit*] *more gross to love vice for itself* [*fell not from heaven*], are two adjective clauses qualifying *Belial.* The construction of the elliptical adverbial clause *than whom* is quite anomalous. No explanation can be given of the objective case in which the relative is used. If a personal pronoun were used, the clause would run: *A spirit more lewd than he* [*was lewd*] *fell not from heaven;* and there is no reason why the relative pronoun should have a different construction. (See *l.* 493.) Under these circumstances, it is useless to attempt to fill up the ellipsis. The clause qualifies *more. To love,* &c., is an adverbial adjunct of *gross.*

l. 493. In analysis leave out *or,* and put in *to him no,* before *altar.* After *who* put in *was. Than he* [*was oft*], an elliptical adverbial clause qualifying *more.* The connective adverb *than,* at the beginning of it, qualifies *oft,* understood. (*Gr.* p. 85; *note* 556, 559.)

l. 498. After *and,* insert *he reigns.*

l. 499. *Of riot, of injury,* and *of outrage,* form three attributive adjuncts of *noise.*

l. 502. This use of *flown* is not easy of explanation. It seems to be used in the sense of *inflated.*

l. 503. In full: *Let the streets of Sodom witness, and let that night in Gibeah witness. Genesis* xix. 1—11; *Judges* xix. 22.

l. 507. *Long* is the complement of the predicate *were,* and *to tell* is in the adverbial relation to *long. The rest* is the subject of the sentence. *To tell* is used in its original sense of *to count.* So *tale* means *a number,* as when we read of *the tale of bricks, we spend our years as a tale that is told, i.e.,* as a number which is counted off, *one, two, three,* &c. After *though,* insert *they were.*

l. 508. Javan was the son of Japheth (*Gen.* x. 2), and the ancestor of the Ionian race. *Of Javan's issue* forms an attributive adjunct of *gods,* and *gods* is in apposition to *the rest.* After *parents* supply *were late.* The clause, *Than—parents* [*were late*], qualifies the adverb *later.*

l. 510. Properly speaking, Titan was not the name of any one divinity. (See *note* on *l.* 197.) It is not easy to see how *Titan* is to be constructed, unless we supply after it *was far renowned.*

l. 515. Ida is the Cretan mountain. Zeus was said to have been born and reared in the Dictæan cave, which was in the Cretan range of mountains. *On the snowy top of cold Olympus* may be taken as an adverbial adjunct of *ruled*, of which *these* is the subject.

l. 517. After *cliff, Dodona*, and *land*, supply *these ruled the middle air*. Apollo was specially worshipped at Delphi, Zeus at Dodona in Epirus.

l. 519. *Who with—isles*. A compound adjective clause qualifying an antecedent understood, the construction of which, if expressed, is not very obvious. The whole passage is excessively harsh and irregular.

l. 520. The Italian agricultural divinity Saturnus had nothing whatever to do with the Grecian Cronus. The only reason why they were subsequently identified seems to have been that they were both very ancient divinities. Saturnus was properly the god of plenty. The name is derived from *satur*—full. Ops (*abundance*) was his wife.

l. 521. *The Celtic* probably means the *Celtic ocean*.

l. 522. After *all these* supply *came flocking*. After *but* put in *they came flocking*.

l. 523. *Such wherein*. There is no way of making these words hang together, except by expanding *such* into *with such looks*. The clause *wherein—loss itself* will then be an adjective clause qualifying *looks*, and co-ordinate with *such*. (*Gr.* 412.)

l. 524. The two phrases beginning with *to have found*, form attributive adjuncts of *joy*. (*Gr.* 362, 4.)

l. 526. *Which* seems to relate not to any particular word, but to the general idea suggested by the previous passage. For analysis it may be replaced by *and these conflicting feelings*, or something of the kind.

l. 529. *Not substance*. In full: *that did not bear substance of worth*.

l. 530. Before *dispelled* insert *he his wonted—substance*.

l. 534. *As his right*. An elliptical adverbial clause, qualifying *claimed*. In full: *as* [*he would claim*] *his right*.

l. 537. *Like* may be taken either as an adjective qualifying *which* (as though equivalent to *resembling*), or as an adverb (*similiter*), qualifying *shone*. In either case it is itself qualified by the adverbial phrase [*to*] *a meteor*, &c.

l. 538. *Rich* is here used adverbially. [*With*] *seraphic arms* and [*with seraphic*] *trophies*, are adverbial adjuncts of *emblazed*.

l. 540. *Metal blowing*, &c. A nominative absolute, forming an adverbial adjunct of *unfurled*.

l. 541. *At which—night.* A compound adjective clause, not qualifying any substantive in particular, but referring generally to the act described in the preceding passage. For analysis substitute *and at this.* *Reign* is used in the sense of *realm* (Lat. *regnum*).

l. 544. *All.* An adverb qualifying the adverbial phrase *in a moment.*

l. 545. Milton uses *rise* (without *to*) after the passive verb, just as it is used after the active; as, *I saw him rise.* It forms the complement of the predicate *were seen.*

l. 549. After *innumerable* repeat *appeared.*

l. 550. The *Dorian mood* was a particular key or scale adopted by the Dorians for their melodies, and depending partly upon the pitch or key-note of the scale, and partly upon the musical intervals between the successive notes of it.

l. 551. *Such* agrees with *mood,* and is co-ordinate with the elliptical adjective sentence, *as* [*the mood was which*] *raised—battle and which instead—retreat.* (*Gr.* 412.)

l. 555. *To flight* and *to foul retreat,* form adverbial adjuncts of *unmoved.*

l. 556. *Wanting* agrees with *mood.* *To mitigate, to swage, to chase,* &c., form attributive adjuncts of *power.* *Swage* (commonly *assuage*) is derived from the Latin *suavis.* So *diluvium* gives rise to *deluge.*

l. 562. *O'er the burnt soil* is an attributive adjunct of *steps.*

l. 563. *Front* is in apposition to *they.*

l. 566. It is, perhaps, best to take *what* as an interrogative pronoun. The clause *what—impose* will then be a substantive clause, the object of *awaiting.*

l. 568. *Traverse;* that is, *transversely.* With each of the objects, *order, visages,* and *stature,* repeat *he views.*

l. 570. *As of gods.*

l. 573. *For never,* &c. This sentence goes on to *l.* 587. It should be attached to the predicate of *each* of the preceding sentences, *distends* and *glories.*

Since created man. That is, *since man was created.* An imitation of the Latin idiom *post urbem conditam, ante me consulem,* &c.

l. 574. The elliptical adjective clause *as named—cranes* explains *such.* In full it is: *as* [*the force would be which*] *named with these could merit more than that small infantry warred on by cranes* [*could merit much*]. The subordinate adverbial clause *than—cranes* qualifies *more.* (*Gr.* 547, 553.)

l. 575. Milton here refers to the Pygmaei, a fabulous race of tin dwarfs, a cubit high, mentioned by Homer (*Il.* iii. 5) as dwelling on the shores of Oceanus, where they had yearly to carry on a fight with the cranes. Other writers located them on the banks of the Nile, in the extreme north, or to the east of the Ganges.

l. 576. *Though all—gods.* An adverbial clause of concession, qualifying *met.*

l. 577. The Gigantes, or Earth-born (see note on *l.* 197) were fabled to have been born in the plains of Phlegra. The name indicates a volcanic district of some kind. Conflicting accounts fix this region in Sicily, Macedonia, and Campania.

l. 579. *Mixed* agrees with *that,* the subject of the verb *fought.* The reader of Greek mythology will remember that various gods took different sides in the Trojan war, and the war of the Seven against Thebes.

Before *what* insert *with.* The clause *what resounds—knights,* is an adjective clause used substantively, and governed by *with.* The whole phrase [*with*] *what—knights,* forms another adverbial adjunct of *were joined.* The construction of the passage is more definite than its sense.

l. 580. *Uther's son.* King Arthur. Armorica obtained its name of Bretagne or Brittany from the British tribes, who retreated thither before the Saxons, and carried with them the legends of King Arthur, who is quite as much an Armorican as a British hero.

l. 582. Before *all* insert *with. With all,* &c., forms another adverbial adjunct of *were joined. Who since,* &c., subdivides itself into the following clauses:—1. *Who since, baptized, jousted in Aspramont.* 2, 3, 4, 5. The same clause repeated, with the substitution (successively) of *Montalban, Damasco, Marocco,* and *Trebizond,* for *Aspramont.* Then all these five clauses must be repeated, with the substitution of *infidel* for *baptized.* We thus get ten adjective clauses qualifying *all.* Aspramont was a town in the Netherlands. Montalban was on the borders of Languedoc. Trebizond (the ancient Trapezus) is connected with the exploits of St. George.

l. 585. Before *whom* supply *though all the giant brood of Phlegra were joined with those.* Fontarabia was a town in Biscay. The Saracens crossed into Spain from Biserta in Africa. This account of the death of Charlemagne rests on Spanish authority only. French writers represent him as victorious.

l. 587. *These* is the subject of the sentence. The phrase *beyond compare of* (i.e., *comparison with*) *mortal prowess* forms an attributive adjunct of *these,* and is itself qualified by *thus far.*

l. 591. *Like a tower.* See note on *l.* 537.

l. 592. *Nor appeared.* That is, *and his form appeared not.* *Less* is the complement of *appeared*, and is qualified by the elliptical adverbial clauses *than Archangel ruined* [*would appear great*], and *than the excess of glory obscured* [*would appear great*].

l. 594. Before *as* supply *his form appeared;* and after *as* supply *the sun appears.*

l. 596. After *or* supply *his form appeared as the sun appears when he.*

l. 598. Before *with* put in *when he.*

l. 601. *Intrenched.* That is, *furrowed.* French, *trancher.*

l. 602. Before *under* repeat *care sat.*

l. 604. After *cruel* put in *was*, and repeat *his eye* before *cast.*

l. 605. *To behold—in pain.* An adverbial adjunct of *cast.* *To behold* is equivalent to *at beholding.*

l. 606. *The followers rather.* This had better be taken as an elliptical parenthesis [*they should be called*] *the followers rather.*

l. 609. *Millions*, &c. This may be taken as a noun in apposition to *fellows*, or we may repeat before it, *his eye cast signs of remorse and passion to behold.*

l. 611. It would be as well to repeat *to behold* before *how.* We thus get another adverbial adjunct of *cast* (*l.* 604). The clause *how they*, &c., will then be a substantive clause, the object of *behold.*

l. 612. *Their glory withered.* A nominative absolute, in the adverbial relation to *stood.*

As—heath. A compound adverbial clause qualifying *stood.* The subject of it is *growth*, the predicate *stands.* To fill up the ellipse first leave out *or mountain pines*, and next repeat the whole, substituting *mountain pines* for *forest oaks.*

l. 614. *Though* [*they be*] *bare.* An adverbial clause qualifying *stands.*

l. 616. *Whereat* must be taken as equivalent to *and at this.*

l. 620. *As* [*tears are which*] *angels weep.* An elliptical adjective clause co-ordinate with *such.* (See *Gr.* 412.)

l. 623. *But with the Almighty.* An adverbial phrase qualifying *matchless.* It is itself made up of a preposition *but* (see *Gr.* 504), governing (apparently) another adverbial phrase, as in *never but now*, *anywhere but here*, and so forth. The adverb or adverbial phrase after *but* should be expanded into some kind of *substantive* expression.

l. 625. Repeat *as* after *and*, and *testifies* after *utter.*

l. 629. After *gods* supply *could ever know repulse.* The next clause, *how such* [*beings*] *as* [*beings were which*] *stood like these—repulse*, will form another object of *feared:* or the whole sentence may be repeated with each clause.

l. 631. Supply *it be* after *though.*

l. 633. *To re-ascend,* &c., may be taken as the object of *fail.*

l. 635. *Be* need not be taken as an imperative. It is a subjunctive, with the force of the Greek optative.

l. 636. After *different* insert *have lost our hopes;* and after *or* repeat *if.*

l. 638. *Till then.* See *note* on *l.* 623. After *secure* supply *sits.* Repeat *he who reigns—upheld by* before *consent,* and *custom.*

l. 641. Repeat *he who—till then* before *put* and before *still.*

l. 642. *Which* does not relate to any one word in the preceding sentence. Treat it as equivalent to *and this.*

l. 643. In full: 1. *Henceforth his might we know so as* [*we should know his might*] *not to* (that is, *in order that we may not*) *provoke new war.* 2. *Henceforth* [*we*] *know our own* [*might*] *so as* [*we should know our own might*] *not to dread new war* [*if we be*] *provoked.*

l. 647. *That he,* &c. An abverbial clause qualifying *to work.* On the construction of the connective adverb *that,* see *Gr.* 528.

l. 648. Before *who* supply *that he.* The clause introduced by this conjunction is a substantive clause, the object of *may find.*

l. 650. *Space* here means *lapse of time.* (Compare *l.* 50.) The clause *whereof—heaven* had better be taken as an adjective clause qualifying *worlds. Whereof* should be taken as an attributive adjunct of the (understood) object of *create,* the import of the sentence being "that he intended to create some worlds of which sort, and therein plant ——— heaven, there went so rife a fame in heaven." The structure of the sentence is very obscure. *Rife* is the complement of the predicate *went.* The clause *that he ere long—heaven* is a substantive clause in apposition to *fame.* An object (*some worlds*) must be supplied after *create. Equal* had better be taken as the complement of *should favour.*

l. 655. *If but to pry.* An elliptical adverbial clause, qualifying *shall be.* In full: *If our eruption be but* (i.e., *only*) *to pry.* Repeat the whole sentence with *elsewhere* instead of *thither,* and in each sentence insert the adverbial clauses: *for this infernal—in bondage,* and *for the abyss shall not long under darkness cover celestial spirits.*

l. 661. Two co-ordinate sentences: 1. *War then open must be resolved.* 2. *War then understood must be resolved.*

l. 673. Before *undoubted* supply *this was an.* The clause *that in his—sulphur* is a substantive clause in apposition to *sign.*

l. 674. In the infancy of chemistry and mineralogy it was imagined that the various metals were produced by the action of sulphur upon mercury, which was regarded as the basis of all metallic matter.

l. 675. *As* [*men hasten*] *when*, &c. An elliptical adverbial clause qualifying *hastened*.

l. 678. Before *east* repeat *when bands of—the royal camp to.*

l. 679. Leave out the second *Mammon* in the analysis. *Spirit*, with its attributive adjective clause, *that fell from heaven*, is in apposition to *Mammon*.

l. 680. *For e'en*, &c. Before this adverbial clause supply some such sentence as *I say least erected*, to the predicate of which it will be attached.

l. 683. *Than* [*he enjoyed much*] *aught*, &c. An elliptical adverbial clause qualifying *more*. The use of *or* necessitates the division of it into two separate clauses, with each of which the whole of the rest of the sentence has to be taken. First leave out *or holy*, and then repeat for *e'en in heaven—beatific*, substituting *holy* for *divine*. (*Gr.* 551, 553.)

l. 690. *Admire*, that is, *wonder*, which is the proper meaning of the word.

l. 692. *Let* (*ye*) is a verb in the imperative mood; *those* is its object, and *learn* its complement. Before *wondering* repeat *who*.

l. 694. *Of Babel* and *of the works*, &c., are adverbial adjuncts of *tell* (*Gr.* p. 101, *note*).

l. 695. *How*, &c. A substantive clause, the object of *learn*. (*Gr.* 403.)

l. 697. After *and* repeat *how*, and after *perform* repeat *is easily outdone by spirits reprobate*.

l. 698. *What—perform*. An adjective clause (*Gr.* 408. *Note* on *l.* 22), used substantively, as the subject of *is outdone*.

l. 703. *Founded*; i.e., *melted*. The two meanings of *found* are derived respectively from *fundere* and *fundare*.

l. 704. Before *scummed* repeat *nigh on—with wondrous art*.

l. 705. *As soon*. *As* is here a demonstrative adverb.

l. 706. Before *from* repeat *a third* [*multitude*].

l. 711. *Like*, &c. See *note* on *l.* 537.

l. 713. *Where*, &c. An adjective clause (*Gr.* 410) qualifying *temple*. *Pilasters and pillars* form a compound subject to *were set*.

l. 716. In full: *There did not want cornice; there did not want frieze—graven*. *Want* is intransitive.

l. 717. *Not Babylon*, &c. Separate this into three sentences: 1, *Babylon equalled not such magnificence in all its glories to enshrine Belus, its god.* 2. *Great Alcairo equalled not—to enshrine Serapis, its god.* 3. *Babylon and Alcairo equalled not such magnificence in all their glories to seat—luxury.* Milton speaks of Alcairo (a city of Arabian origin) as though it were the capital of the Pharaohs.

l. 723. *Her stately height.* An adverbial phrase. (*Gr.* 373, 3.) (Compare *l.* 282.) It qualifies *fixed.*

l. 724. *Discover* here is to *disclose* or *uncover. Wide* and *within* had better be taken as adverbs, qualifying *discover.*

l. 728. *Cressets.* From the French *croisette.*

l. 730. *As* [*they would have yielded light*] *from a sky.* An adverbial clause attached to the predicate *yielded.*

l. 735. Before *sat* repeat *where sceptred angels.* After *princes* insert *sit*, or *would have sat.* The clauses beginning with *where* are adjective clauses (*Gr.* 410) qualifying *structure.*

l. 736. *And* [*to whom the supreme king*] *gave,* &c. This adjective clause, like the one that precedes it, qualifies *angels. To rule—bright* will be the objective adjunct of *gave.* If *gave* be used in the sense of *placed* or *appointed,* then omit the *to* before *whom.* The phrase *to rule,* &c., will then be an adverbial adjunct of *gave.*

l. 737. *Each in his hierarchy.* An elliptical expression. In full: *giving each to rule in his hierarchy the orders bright.*

l. 738. Subdivide this contracted sentence into two. 1. *His name was not unheard in ancient Greece.* 2. *His name was not unadored in ancient Greece.*

l. 747. *For he,* &c. An adverbial clause qualifying *erring.*

l. 748. *Aught* is in the adverbial relation to *availed,* the subject of which is *to have built in heaven high towers.*

l. 755. *To be held,* &c. An attributive adjunct of *council.* (*Gr.* 362, 4.)

l. 757. A contracted sentence—divide it thus: 1. *Their summons called from—regiment the spirits worthiest by place.* 2. *Their summons called from—regiment the spirits worthiest by choice.*

l. 752. After *wide* insert *thick swarmed.*

l. 763. *Though* [*it was*] *like—lance.* An adverbial clause, qualifying the predicate *swarmed.* [*To*] *a covered field* is in the adverbial relation to *like. Covered* here means *listed, enclosed for combat.*

l. 764. *Wont* is here a verb in the indicative mood. *Ride* is its complement.

Before *at* repeat *where champions bold.*

l. 766. Before *career* supply *where champions bold at the Soldan's chair defied the best of Panim chivalry to. Career* is here a noun. *With lance* is an attributive adjunct of *career.*

l. 768. *As bees—affairs.* A contracted compound adverbial clause. qualifying both *swarmed* and *were straitened*, for the second of which it must be repeated.

l. 771. Before *they* insert *as.* The grammatical connection between this sentence and what precedes is not as close as would be convenient.

l. 772. Insert *as they* before *on the smoothed plank.*

l. 774. Before *confer* repeat *as they on the smoothed plank—with balm.*

l. 776. Before *were straitened* repeat the whole clause *as bees—affairs.*

l. 776. *Till behold a wonder.* This of course is not a legitimate construction, grammatically speaking. For analysis substitute *a wonder ensued*, or something of the kind. The clause is in the adverbial relation to *were straitened.*

l. 777. *But now.* *But* here has the sense of *only.*

l. 778. *To surpass*, &c., is the complement of the predicate *seemed.*

l. 779. *Than smallest dwarfs* [*are little*]. An elliptical adverbial clause, qualifying *less.* (*Gr.* 553.)

l. 780. *Like* had better be taken as an adjective, qualifying *they.* (See *l.* 575.)

l. 781. Before *faery* repeat *they but now—numberless, like.*

l. 782. A compound contracted adjective clause. First leave out *or fountain* and *or dreams he sees.* Next repeat the sentence so formed, with the substitution of *fountain* for *forest-side.* Thirdly, repeat *each* of these sentences with the substitution of *dreams he sees* for *sees.*

l. 784. [*That*] *he sees*, &c. A substantive clause, the object of *dreams.* *Revels*, with its adjuncts, will now belong to this substantive clause.

l. 785. Before *nearer* repeat *while over head the moon.*

l. 791. After *though* insert *they were.*

l. 793. *In their own dimensions.* An attributive adjunct of *lords* and *cherubim.*

l. 796. *On golden seats* may be taken either as an attributive adjunct of *demigods*, or as an adverbial adjunct of *sitting*, understood.

A LIST OF DIFFICULT WORDS,

ESPECIALLY SUCH AS ARE USED IN OBSOLETE OR UNUSUAL SENSES.

Abject (*abjicio, abjectus*), cast aside. (*l.* 312.)
Abuse (*abutor, abusus sum*), to misuse, to deal with wrongly or unfairly. Hence, to delude or deceive. (*l.* 479.)
Abyss (*ἄβυσσος*), a *bottomless* pit.
Access (*accedo, accessus*), way of approach. (*l.* 761.)
Admire (*admiror*), to wonder. (*l.* 690.)
Advanced (French, *avancer*; Latin, *ab ante*), improved. (*l.* 119.)
Afflicted (*affligo*), dashed down. (*l.* 186.)
Affront (*ad, frons*), to meet face to face. (*l.* 391.)
Aim (*aestimo*), object intended. (*l.* 168.)
Amerce (French, *à merci*; Latin, *ad misericordiam*), to impose a fine at the discretion, or *mercy*, of the court,—not a fine fixed by law. (*l.* 609.)
Ammiral (Arabic, *amir*, 'a lord'). A *chief* of any kind. A commander of a fleet; hence the commander's *ship*. (*l.* 294.) 'Admiral' is a corruption of the word.
Arch (*ἀρχή*), leading or governing. *Arch*angel, *arch*-fiend, &c. (*l.* 156.)
Architrave (*ἀρχός, trabs*), the lower division of an entablature, the part resting on the column. The entablature is made up of architrave, frieze, and cornice. (*l.* 715.)
Argument (*arguo, argumentum*), subject for discussion. (*l.* 24.)
Astonished (*attonitus*), thunderstruck. (*l.* 307.)

Balance (*bi-lanx*). 'In even balance,' *i.e.*, 'poising themselves evenly on their wings.' (*l.* 349.) Compare II., *l.* 1046.
Beatific (*beatus, facio*), making happy. (*l.* 684.)
Beneath, still lower than—still more degrading than—(*l.* 115.) Also 'to the South of.' (*l.* 355.)
Bestial (*bestia, bestialis*), in the *form* of beasts. (*l.* 435).

Bordering, forming a border or boundary. (*l.* 419.)
Bossy, projecting; from 'boss,' a 'knob or protuberance.' (*l.* 716.)
Bullion (*bulla*, 'a seal or stamp'), anciently signified the *mint*, where gold and silver were reduced to *stamped* money. Afterwards it signified the *alloy* which was permitted by the Bullion or Mint, and so it came to mean all gold and silver designed for coinage, or coined. (*l.* 704.)

Camp, army. (*l.* 677.)
Chivalry (*caballus*), cavalry, a body of knights. (*l.* 307.)
Choice (used actively), distinguishing. (*l.* 653.)
Clime (κλίμα, 'a slope'), properly 'the *slope* of the earth from the equator towards the poles.' Hence 'a *zone* or *belt* of the earth.' (*l.* 242. Comp. *l.* 297.)
Combustible (*comburo*), capable of burning. (*l.* 233.)
Combustion, destruction by fire. (*l.* 46.)
Conceive (*concipio*), to catch. 'I *conceive* your meaning' means 'I *catch* your meaning *thoroughly*.' (*l.* 234.)
Conclave (*conclave; con clavis*), a locked apartment, a close or private meeting. (*l.* 795.)
Conduct (*conduco*), guidance. (*l.* 130.)
Confer (*confero*), to bring together for discussion. (*l.* 774.)
Considerate (*considero*), reflecting, contemplative, not rash or hasty. Used actively. (*l.* 603.)
Consult used as a noun (*consultum*), consultation. (*l.* 798.)
Contention (*contendo, contentio*), struggle. (*l.* 100.)
Cope (*cupa*, 'a bowl'), an arched covering. (*l.* 345.)
Cornice (κορωνίς), a summit or finish; the uppermost part of an entablature. (*l.* 716.)
Crew, a band of comrades. (*l.* 51.)

Damp, chilled, depressed. (*l.* 523.) 'Damped' is more commonly used in this sense.
Deify (*deus, facio*), to worship or reverence as divine. (*l.* 112.)
Different (*differo*), differing, divided, at variance with each other. (*l.* 636.)
Dilated (*differo, dilatus*), expanded. (*l.* 429.)
Discover (*dis, co-operire*), to uncover, to reveal to sight. (*ll.* 64, 724.)
Dispose (*dispono*), to arrange. (*l.* 246.)
Double (*duplicare*), to repeat. (*l.* 485.)
Doubt (*dubitare*), to think insecure. (*l.* 114.)
Doubtful hue, a mixed expression, partly of one kind, partly of another. (*l.* 527.)
Dread, an object of fear. (*l.* 406.)
Dreadful, inspiring terror. (*l.* 130.)
Dubious (*dubius*), doubtful, not instantly decided. (*l.* 104.)
Dulcet (*dulcis*), sweet-sounding. (*l.* 712.)

Emblaze, to adorn with bright or flaming colours. (*l.* 539.) The form *emblazon* is now usually employed.

Emperor (*imperator*), commander. (*l.* 378.)

Empyreal (*ἔμπυρος*), dwelling in the region of fire. (*l.* 117.) See *Ethereal.*

Endure (*indurare*), to harden one's self, to hold out. (*l.* 299.)

Enlarge, to cause to spread. (*l.* 415.)

Envy (*invidia*), grudging, strong desire to have for oneself. (*l.* 260.) 'Hath not built here for his envy;' *i.e.*, hath not built here a dwelling that he would strongly desire for himself.

Equal (*æqualis*), to place on the same level with. (*l.* 284.) 'To equal which' (*l.* 292) means 'in comparison with which,' placed side by side with it, to see if it is of equal length. Also, to lay all equally low. (*l.* 488.)

Erst, formerly; the superlative answering to the comparative *ere.* (*l.* 360.)

Eruption (*eruptio*), a breaking forth, a sally. (*l.* 656.)

Essences (*esse*, modern Latin *essentia*), natures, beings. (*l.* 138.)

Ethereal (*aethereus*; *αἰθήρ*, 'blazing heat'), belonging to the region of the ether, *i.e.*, heavenly (*ll.* 45, 285.) By *aether* the ancients understood the upper, pure, glowing air, beyond the region of mists and clouds (which they called *ἀήρ*); a rare and fiery medium in which the heavenly bodies moved.

Event (*eventus*), the result of a course of action. (*l.* 118.)

Expatiate (*ex*, *spatior*), to strut about. (*l.* 774.)

Fail, to lose strength, to perish; to be mistaken. (*ll.* 117, 167.)

Fame (*fama*), report. (*l.* 651.)

Fanatic (*fanaticus*, *fanum*), inspired or possessed by a divinity, furious, mad. (*l.* 480.)

Fast, close. (*l.* 12.)

Flown, elated, puffed up, flushed. (*l.* 502.) *Flown* is properly the participle of *fly*, but it is difficult to trace the meaning, as derived from this verb. If Milton connected it with *flow*, *flown* may have much the same sense as *flooded.*

Flung, banished. (*l.* 610.)

Found (*fundĕre*), to melt, to pour. (*l.* 703.)

Founded (*fundāre*), established, fixed firmly. (*l.* 427.)

Foundered—'Some small night-foundered skiff.' It is very difficult to trace the exact sense of this phrase. Bentley even suggested *nigh-foundered*, i.e., *almost sinking.* *Founder* ('to sink') is derived from the old French verb *afondrer* (*ad*, *fundus*), 'to sink to the bottom.' From the Latin *fundere* we get a verb *founder* of very similar meaning, implying *to melt, sink, give way, fall.* (In French *se fondre*). In old English it is applied to a horse stumbling. In Jamieson's Scottish Dictionary we find *founder* in the sense of *to fell, to knock down, to give a stunning blow.*

Frequent (*frequens*), crowded. (*l.* 797.)
Fretted, divided into squares or lozenges by interlacing or intersecting bars (*laqueatus*). It appears to be derived from *ferrum*, through the Italian *ferrata*, 'an iron grating.'
Frieze, the embossed or ornamented border running beneath the cornice of an entablature. (*l.* 716.)
Fuelled (*focus, focale*), charged or loaded with fuel. (*l.* 234.)
Fury (*furor*), violent action. 'Mineral fury,' the violent action with which sulphur, nitre, and such mineral products burn, or act and react on each other. (*l.* 235.) See *Mineral.*

Graze, to feed or supply with grass. (*l.* 486.) The verb is now commonly applied to the pasture (to eat off the grass), not to the cattle that feed upon it. 'To graze' (in Milton's sense) is now commonly expressed by 'to pasture.'
Grunsel, *i.e.*, *ground-sill*, the threshold. (*l.* 460.)

Heat, passionate or burning love. (*l.* 453.)
Homicide (*homicida ; homo caedo*), used adjectively. 'manslaying.' (*l.* 417.)

Incumbent (*incumbo*), resting his weight upon. (*l.* 226.)
Infernal (*inferi*), belonging to Hell. (*l.* 34.)
Inflamed (*inflammatus*), blazing, set on fire. (*l.* 300.)
Injured (*injuria*), treated with injustice, meeting with less than justice. (*l.* 98.)
Intrench (French *trancher* ; Latin *truncare*, 'to lop off'), to cut trenches or furrows in anything.
Invest (*in, vestis*), to throw a robe or cloak over. (*l.* 208.)
Involved (*involvĕre*), enveloped, wrapped up. (*l.* 236.)

Ken, to know, to perceive. (*l.* 59.)

Light, to alight. (*l.* 228.)
Lucid (*lux, lucidus*), bright, letting light pass through. (*l.* 469.)

Mansion (*mansio, manēre*), a dwelling-place, not necessarily a building of any kind.
Measure (*mensura, metior*), treatment, what is *meted* out to a person. (*l.* 513.)
Middle (*medius*), between two extremes, not reaching the *highest* point. (*l.* 14.)
Mineral, found in mines, or under the earth. 'Mineral fury' (*l.* 235) perhaps means merely 'violent subterranean action.'
Mortal (*mors, mortalis*), deadly, causing death. (*l.* 2). Also employed in the sense of 'exposed to death.'
Myriad (μυρίας), properly, a body of ten thousand. (*l.* 87.)

Nathless (*i.e.*, *na-the-less*), nevertheless. (*l.* 299.)

Obdurate (*ob*, *durus*), hardened against everything. (*l.* 58.)
Oblivious (*obliviosus*), causing forgetfulness. (*l.* 266.)
Offend (*offendo*), to assail or attack. (*l.* 187.)
Offensive, causing disgrace. The 'offensive mountain' (*l.* 443) is the same as the 'opprobrious hill' (*l.* 403), called also the 'hill of scandal.' (*l.* 416.)
Orgies (*orgia*), wild, frenzied ceremonies. (*l.* 415.)
Orient (*orior*), connected with sunrise. 'Orient colours' are the bright colours of sunrise. (*l.* 546.)

Part (*pars*), share or portion. (*l.* 267.)
Passion (*patior*, *passio*), suffering. (*l.* 605.)
Penal (*pœna*), endured by way of punishment. (*l.* 48.)
Perdition (*perdo*), utter ruin. 'Bottomless perdition' (*l.* 47), the bottomless pit of ruin.
Pernicious (*pernicies*, *perniciosus*), deadly, destructive. (*l.* 282.)
Pilaster (*pila*), a square pillar, usually let into a wall, so as to project only by a portion of its thickness. (*l.* 713.)
Precipice (*praeceps*), the extreme verge, from which one can fall headlong. (*l.* 173.)
Presage (*prae*, *sapio*), to know beforehand. (*l.* 627.)
Prime (*primus*), foremost. (*l.* 506.)
Profane (*pro*, *fanum*), to treat as not being sacred. A thing is *profane* which is *pro fano*, in front of, or outside the sacred enclosure. (*l.* 390.)
Prone (*pronus*), headlong, lying flat. (*l.* 195.)
Providence (*providēre*), foresight. (*l.* 162.)
Puissant (French *je puis*), powerful. (*l.* 632.)
Pursue (*pro*, *sequor*), to follow out, to go along with, to treat of continuously. (*l.* 15.)

Recollect (*recolligo*), to gather up again. (*l.* 528.)
Recorder, a kind of wind instrument. (*l.* 551.)
Reign (*regnum*), kingdom, realm. (*l.* 543.)
Reinforcement, renewal of strength. (*l.* 190.)
Religions (*religiones*), religious rites. (*l.* 372.)
Re-possess (*re-possidēre*), to re-occupy. (*l.* 634.)
Rife, prevalent, abundant. (*l.* 650.)
Rout, a gang or crowd. (*l.* 747.) Probably not of the same origin as *rout*, applied to an army. The latter is connected with *ruptus*, 'broken.'
Ruin (*ruina*), sudden downfall. (*l.* 46.)

Satiate (*satiatus*, *satis*), satisfied, satiated. (*l.* 179.)
Scandal (σκάνδαλον), a stumbling-block, an offence or disgrace. (*l.* 416.) See *Offensive*.

Scum (verb), to skim. (*l.* 704.)
Secret (*secretus*), retired, withdrawn from public gaze. (*l.* 6.)
Secure (*securus*), free from anxiety. (*l.* 261.)
Serried (French, *serrer*), locked together. (*l.* 548.)
Shrine (*scrinium*), a box or chest enclosing something sacred, like the Ark in the Jewish temple. (*l.* 388.)
Slip, to let slip. (*l.* 178.)
Sluiced, poured through sluices. (*l.* 702.) *Sluice* (derived from *exclusa*), implies a floodgate, by which the water is *shut off*.
Space (*spatium*), period of time. (*l.* 50.)
Spires (σπεῖρα), tapering jets. (*l.* 223.) The word properly implies something *twisted*.
Straiten (*strictus*), to crowd into a narrow space. (*l.* 776.)
Sublimed (*sublimis*), driven off in vapour. A chemical phrase. (*l.* 235).
Successful, involving better auguries of success. (*l.* 120.)
Suffice (*sufficio*), to satisfy. (*l.* 148.)
Supernal (*supernus*), belonging to the supreme (or, at least, some exalted) being. (*l.* 241.)
Suppliant (*supplicari*), bending low. (*l.* 112.)
Sure (*securus*), inspiring confidence. (*l.* 278.)
Symphony (σὺν, φωνή), a union of notes or voices. (*l.* 712.)

Temper (*temperare*), the mode in which the ingredients of a compound are proportioned to each other. (*l.* 285.)
Tend (*tendo*), to direct one's course. (*l.* 183.)
Thrall, slave. (*l.* 149.)
Torrid (*torridus*), scorching. (*l.* 297.)
Transcendent (*transcendere*), climbing beyond, surpassing ordinary limits. (*l.* 86.)
Traverse (*transversus*), transversely. (*l.* 568.)

Unfrequented (*frequens*). 'To frequent' means 'to visit in crowds.' *Frequens senatus* is, 'a crowded meeting of the senate.' (*l.* 433.)
Unsung, not celebrated in song, or poetry. (*l.* 442.)
Urge (*urgeo*), to press upon, or afflict. (*l.* 68.)
Utter, outer. (*l.* 72.)
Uxorious (*uxor*), passionately devoted to his wives. (*l.* 444.)

Vex (*vexare*), to harass or assail. (*l.* 306.)

Warping, moving forward with an oblique or zigzag motion. (*l.* 341.)
Watch, to keep awake. (*l.* 332.)
Welter (A.-S. *waeltan*), to roll or tumble, especially in anything foul or unclean. (*l.* 78.)
Wont (verb), were accustomed. (*l.* 764.)

PARADISE LOST.

BOOK II.

HIGH on a throne of royal state, which far
Outshone the wealth of Ormus or of Ind,
Or where the gorgeous East with richest hand
Show'rs on her kings barbaric pearl and gold,
Satan exalted sat, by merit raised
To that bad eminence ; and from despair
Thus high uplifted beyond hope aspires
Beyond thus high, insatiate to pursue
Vain war with heav'n, and by success untaught
His proud imaginations thus displayed.
'Pow'rs and dominions, deities of heaven,
For since no deep within her gulf can hold
Immortal vigour, though oppress'd and fall'n
I give not heav'n for lost. From this descent
Celestial virtues rising, will appear
More glorious and more dread than from no fall,
And trust themselves to fear no second fate.
Me though just right, and the fix'd laws of heaven,
Did first create your leader, next free choice,
With what besides, in counsel, or in fight,
Hath been achiev'd of merit, yet this loss
Thus far at least recover'd, hath much more
Establish'd in a safe unenvied throne,
Yielded with full consent. The happier state
In heaven, which follows dignity, might draw
Envy from each inferior ; but who here
Will envy whom the highest place exposes

Foremost to stand against the Thund'rer's aim
Your bulwark, and condemns to greatest share
Of endless pain? where there is then no good
For which to strive, no strife can grow up there
From faction; for none sure will claim in hell
Precedence, none, whose portion is so small
Of present pain, that with ambitious mind
Will covet more. With this advantage then
To union, and firm faith, and firm accord,
More than can be in heav'n, we now return
To claim our just inheritance of old,
Surer to prosper than prosperity
Could have assur'd us; and by what best way,
Whether of open war or covert guile,
We now debate; who can advise, may speak.'
  He ceas'd, and next him Moloch, sceptred king,
Stood up, the strongest and the fiercest Spirit
That fought in heav'n, now fiercer by despair.
His trust was with th' Eternal to be deem'd
Equal in strength, and rather than be less
Car'd not to be at all; with that care lost
Went all his fear: of God, or hell, or worse
He reck'd not, and these words thereafter spake.
  'My sentence is for open war: of wiles,
More unexpert, I boast not: them let those
Contrive who need, or when they need, not now.
For while they sit contriving, shall the rest,
Millions that stand in arms, and longing wait
The signal to ascend, sit ling'ring here
Heav'n's fugitives, and for their dwelling-place
Accept this dark opprobrious den of shame,
The prison of his tyranny who reigns
By our delay? No, let us rather choose,
Arm'd with hell flames and fury, all at once,
O'er heaven's high towers to force resistless way,
Turning our tortures into horrid arms
Against the torturer; when to meet the noise
Of his almighty engine he shall hear

Infernal thunder; and for lightning, see
Black fire and horror shot with equal rage
Among his angels; and his throne itself
Mix'd with Tartarean sulphur, and strange fire,
His own invented torments. But perhaps
The way seems difficult and steep to scale
With upright wing against a higher foe.
Let such bethink them, if the sleepy drench
Of that forgetful lake benumb not still,
That in our proper motion we ascend
Up to our native seat: descent and fall
To us is adverse. Who but felt of late,
When the fierce foe hung on our broken rear
Insulting, and pursued us through the deep,
With what compulsion and laborious flight
We sunk thus low? The ascent is easy then;
The event is fear'd; should we again provoke
Our stronger, some worse way his wrath may find
To our destruction; if there be in hell
Fear to be worse destroy'd. What can be worse
Than to dwell here, driven out from bliss, condemned
In this abhorred deep to utter woe;
Where pain of unextinguishable fire
Must exercise us without hope of end,
The vassals of his anger, when the scourge
Inexorable, and the torturing hour,
Calls us to penance? More destroyed than thus
We should be quite abolish'd, and expire.
What fear we then? what doubt we to incense
His utmost ire? which, to the height enraged,
Will either quite consume us, and reduce
To nothing this essential; happier far
Than miserable to have eternal being:
Or, if our substance be indeed divine,
And cannot cease to be, we are at worst
On this side nothing; and by proof we feel
Our power sufficient to disturb his heaven,
And with perpetual inroads to alarm,

Though inaccessible, his fatal throne:
Which, if not victory, is yet revenge.'
He ended frowning, and his look denounced
Desperate revenge, and battle dangerous
To less than gods. On the other side up rose
Belial, in act more graceful and humane:
A fairer person lost not heaven; he seem'd
For dignity composed, and high exploit:
But all was false and hollow: though his tongue
Dropt manna, and could make the worse appear
The better reason, to perplex and dash
Maturer counsels: for his thoughts were low,
To vice industrious, but to nobler deeds
Timorous and slothful; yet he pleased the ear,
And with persuasive accent thus began:
'I should be much for open war, O peers,
As not behind in hate; if what was urged
Main reason to persuade immediate war,
Did not dissuade me most, and seem to cast
Ominous conjecture on the whole success;
When he, who most excels in fact of arms,
In what he counsels, and in what excels;
Mistrustful grounds his courage on despair
And utter dissolution, as the scope
Of all his aim, after some dire revenge.
First, what revenge? The towers of heaven are fill'd
With armed watch, that render all access
Impregnable: oft on the bordering deep
Encamp their legions; or, with obscure wing,
Scout far and wide into the realm of night,
Scorning surprise. Or could we break our way
By force, and at our heels all hell should rise
With blackest insurrection, to confound
Heaven's purest light; yet our great enemy,
All incorruptible, would on his throne
Sit unpolluted: and the ethereal mould,
Incapable of stain, would soon expel
Her mischief, and purge off the baser fire,

Victorious. Thus repulsed, our final hope
Is flat despair: we must exasperate
The almighty Victor to spend all his rage,
And that must end us; that must be our cure,
To be no more. Sad cure! for who would lose,
Though full of pain, this intellectual being,
Those thoughts that wander through eternity,
To perish rather, swallow'd up and lost
In the wide womb of uncreated night,
Devoid of sense and motion? And who knows,
Let this be good, whether our angry foe
Can give it, or will ever? How he can,
Is doubtful; that he never will, is sure.
Will he, so wise, let loose at once his ire,
Belike through impotence, or unaware,
To give his enemies their wish, and end
Them in his anger, whom his anger saves
To punish endless? Wherefore cease we then?
Say they who counsel war, We are decreed,
Reserved, and destined, to eternal woe;
Whatever doing, what can we suffer more,
What can we suffer worse? Is this then worst,
Thus sitting, thus consulting, thus in arms?
What, when we fled amain, pursued, and struck
With heaven's afflicting thunder, and besought
The deep to shelter us? this hell then seem'd
A refuge from those wounds; or when we lay
Chain'd on the burning lake? that sure was worse.
What if the breath, that kindled those grim fires,
Awaked, should blow them into sevenfold rage,
And plunge us in the flames? or, from above,
Should intermitted vengeance arm again
His red right hand to plague us? What if all
Her stores were open'd, and this firmament
Of hell should spout her cataracts of fire,
Impendent horrors, threatening hideous fall
One day upon our heads; while we perhaps,
Designing or exhorting glorious war,

Caught in a fiery tempest shall be hurl'd
Each on his rock transfix'd, the sport and prey
Of wracking whirlwinds; or for ever sunk
Under yon boiling ocean, wrapt in chains;
There to converse with everlasting groans,
Unrespited, unpitied, unreprieved,
Ages of hopeless end? This would be worse.
War therefore, open or conceal'd, alike
My voice dissuades; for what can force or guile
With him, or who deceive his mind, whose eye
Views all things at one view? He from heaven's height
All these our motions vain, sees, and derides:
Not more almighty to resist our might,
Than wise to frustrate all our plots and wiles.
Shall we then live thus vile, the race of heaven
Thus trampled, thus expell'd to suffer here
Chains and these torments? Better these than worse,
By my advice; since fate inevitable
Subdues us, and omnipotent decree,
The victor's will. To suffer, as to do,
Our strength is equal, nor the law unjust
That so ordains: this was at first resolved,
If we were wise, against so great a foe
Contending, and so doubtful what might fall.
I laugh, when those who at the spear are bold
And venturous, if that fail them, shrink and fear
What yet they know must follow, to endure
Exile, or ignominy, or bonds, or pain,
The sentence of their conqueror. This is now
Our doom; which if we can sustain and bear,
Our supreme foe in time may much remit
His anger; and perhaps, thus far removed,
Not mind us not offending, satisfied
With what is punish'd; whence these raging fires
Will slacken, if his breath stir not their flames:
Our purer essence then will overcome
Their noxious vapour, or, inured, not feel;
Or, changed at length, and to the place conform'd

In temper and in nature, will receive
Familiar the fierce heat, and void of pain;
This horror will grow mild, this darkness light;
Besides what hope the never-ending flight
Of future days may bring, what chance, what change
Worth waiting; since our present lot appears
For happy though but ill, for ill not worst,
If we procure not to ourselves more woe.'
Thus Belial, with words clothed in reason's garb,
Counsell'd ignoble ease, and peaceful sloth,
Not peace; and after him thus Mammon spake:
'Either to disenthrone the King of heaven
We war, if war be best, or to regain
Our own right lost: him to unthrone we then
May hope, when everlasting fate shall yield
To fickle chance, and Chaos judge the strife:
The former, vain to hope, argues as vain
The latter: for what place can be for us
Within heaven's bound, unless heaven's Lord supreme
We overpower? Suppose he should relent,
And publish grace to all, on promise made
Of new subjection; with what eyes could we
Stand in his presence humble, and receive
Strict laws imposed, to celebrate his throne
With warbled hymns, and to his Godhead sing
Forced hallelujahs; while he lordly sits
Our envied sovereign, and his altar breathes
Ambrosial odours and ambrosial flowers,
Our servile offerings? This must be our task
In heaven, this our delight; how wearisome
Eternity so spent, in worship paid
To whom we hate! Let us not then pursue
By force impossible, by leave obtain'd
Unacceptable, though in heaven, our state
Of splendid vassalage; but rather seek
Our own good from ourselves, and from our own
Live to ourselves, though in this vast recess,
Free, and to none accountable, preferring

Hard liberty, before the easy yoke
Of servile pomp. Our greatness will appear
Then most conspicuous, when great things of small,
Useful of hurtful, prosperous of adverse,
We can create; and in what place soe'er
Thrive under evil, and work ease out of pain,
Through labour and endurance. This deep world
Of darkness do we dread? How oft amidst
Thick clouds and dark doth heaven's all-ruling Sire
Choose to reside, his glory unobscured,
And with the majesty of darkness round
Covers his throne; from whence deep thunders roar
Mustering their rage, and heaven resembles hell.
As he our darkness, cannot we his light
Imitate when we please? This desert soil
Wants not her hidden lustre, gems and gold;
Nor want we skill or art, from whence to raise
Magnificence; and what can heaven show more?
Our torments also may in length of time
Become our elements: these piercing fires
As soft as now severe, our temper changed
Into their temper; which must needs remove
The sensible of pain. All things invite
To peaceful counsels, and the settled state
Of order, how in safety best we may
Compose our present evils, with regard
Of what we are, and were; dismissing quite
All thoughts of war. Ye have what I advise.'
He scarce had finish'd, when such murmur fill'd
The assembly, as when hollow rocks retain
The sound of blustering winds, which all night long
Had roused the sea, now with hoarse cadence lull
Seafaring men o'er-watch'd, whose barque by chance
Or pinnace anchors in a craggy bay
After the tempest: such applause was heard
As Mammon ended, and his sentence pleased
Advising peace: for such another field
They dreaded worse than hell: so much the fear

Of thunder and the sword of Michael
Wrought still within them, and no less desire
To found this nether empire, which might rise
By policy, and long process of time,
In emulation opposite to heaven.
Which when Beelzebub perceived, than whom
Satan except, none higher sat, with grave
Aspect he rose, and in his rising seem'd
A pillar of state; deep on his front engraven
Deliberation sat, and public care;
And princely counsel in his face yet shone,
Majestic, though in ruin: sage he stood
With Atlantean shoulders fit to bear
The weight of mightiest monarchies; his look
Drew audience and attention still as night
Or summer's noontide air, while thus he spake:
'Thrones and imperial powers, offspring of heaven,
Ethereal virtues; or these titles now
Must we renounce, and changing style, be call'd
Princes of hell? for so the popular vote
Inclines here to continue, and build up here
A growing empire? doubtless, while we dream
And know not that the King of heaven hath doom'd
This place our dungeon, not our safe retreat
Beyond his potent arm, to live exempt
From heaven's high jurisdiction, in new league
Banded against his throne, but to remain
In strictest bondage, though thus far removed,
Under the inevitable curb, reserved
His captive multitude! for he, be sure,
In height or depth, still first and last will reign
Sole king, and of his kingdom lose no part
By our revolt; but over hell extend
His empire, and with iron sceptre rule
Us here, as with his golden those in heaven.
What sit we then projecting peace and war?
War hath determined us, and foil'd with loss
Irreparable: terms of peace yet none

Vouchsafed or sought; for what peace will be given
To us enslaved, but custody severe,
And stripes, and arbitrary punishment,
Inflicted? and what peace can we return,
But to our power hostility and hate,
Untamed reluctance, and revenge, though slow
Yet ever plotting how the Conqueror least
May reap his conquest, and may least rejoice
In doing what we most in suffering feel?
Nor will occasion want, nor shall we need
With dangerous expedition to invade
Heaven, whose high walls fear no assault or siege,
Or ambush from the deep. What if we find
Some easier enterprise? There is a place
(If ancient and prophetic fame in heaven
Err not), another world, the happy seat
Of some new race, call'd Man, about this time
To be created like to us, though less
In power and excellence, but favour'd more
Of him who rules above; so was his will
Pronounced among the Gods; and by an oath,
That shook heaven's whole circumference, confirm'd
Thither let us bend all our thoughts, to learn
What creatures there inhabit, of what mould
Or substance, how endued, and what their power,
And where their weakness, how attempted best
By force or subtlety. Though heaven be shut,
And heaven's high Arbitrator sit secure
In his own strength, this place may lie exposed,
The utmost border of his kingdom, left
To their defence who hold it: here perhaps
Some advantageous act may be achieved
By sudden onset: either with hell fire
To waste his whole creation, or possess
All as our own, and drive as we were driven,
The puny habitants, or, if not drive,
Seduce them to our party, that their God
May prove their foe, and with repenting hand

Abolish his own works. This would surpass
Common revenge, and interrupt his joy
In our confusion, and our joy upraise
In his disturbance; when his darling sons,
Hurl'd headlong to partake with us, shall curse
Their frail original, and faded bliss,
Faded so soon. Advise, if this be worth
Attempting, or to sit in darkness here
Hatching vain empires.' Thus Beëlzebub
Pleaded his devilish counsel, first devised
By Satan, and in part proposed; for whence
But from the author of all ill, could spring
So deep a malice, to confound the race
Of mankind in one root, and earth with hell
To mingle and involve, done all to spite
The great Creator? But their spite still serves
His glory to augment. The bold design
Pleased highly those infernal states, and joy
Sparkled in all their eyes: with full assent
They vote: whereat his speech he thus renews:
'Well have ye judged, well ended long debate,
Synod of gods, and, like to what ye are,
Great things resolved, which, from the lowest deep,
Will once more lift us up, in spite of fate,
Nearer our ancient seat: perhaps in view
Of those bright confines, whence, with neighbouring arms
And opportune excursion, we may chance
Re-enter heaven; or else in some mild zone
Dwell not unvisited of heaven's fair light,
Secure; and at the brightening orient beam
Purge off this gloom: the soft delicious air,
To heal the scar of these corrosive fires,
Shall breathe her balm. But first, whom shall we send
In search of this new world? whom shall we find
Sufficient? who shall tempt with wandering feet
The dark, unbottom'd, infinite abyss,
And through the palpable obscure find out
His uncouth way, or spread his aëry flight

Upborne with indefatigable wings,
Over the vast abrupt, ere he arrive
The happy isle? What strength, what art can then
Suffice, or what evasion bear him safe
Through the strict senteries and stations thick
Of angels watching round? Here he had need
All circumspection, and we now no less
Choice in our suffrage? for, on whom we send,
The weight of all and our last hope relies.'
  This said, he sat; and expectation held
His look suspense, awaiting who appear'd
To second or oppose, or undertake,
The perilous attempt: but all sat mute,
Pondering the danger with deep thoughts; and each
In other's countenance read his own dismay,
Astonish'd: none among the choice and prime
Of those heaven-warring champions could be found
So hardy, as to proffer or accept
Alone, the dreadful voyage; till at last
Satan, whom now transcendent glory raised
Above his fellows, with monarchal pride,
Conscious of highest worth, unmoved thus spake:
  'O progeny of heaven, empyreal thrones,
With reason hath deep silence and demur
Seized us, though undismay'd. Long is the way
And hard, that out of hell leads up to light;
Our prison strong; this huge convex of fire,
Outrageous to devour, immures us round
Ninefold; and gates of burning adamant,
Barr'd over us, prohibit all egress.
These pass'd, if any pass, the void profound
Of unessential night receives him next
Wide-gaping, and with utter loss of being
Threatens him, plunged in that abortive gulf.
If thence he 'scape into whatever world,
Or unknown region, what remains him less
Than unknown dangers, and as hard escape?
But I should ill become this throne, O peers

And this imperial sovereignty adorn'd
With splendour, arm'd with power, if aught proposed
And judged of public moment, in the shape
Of difficulty or danger, could deter
Me from attempting. Wherefore do I assume
These royalties, and not refuse to reign,
Refusing to accept as great a share
Of hazard as of honour, due alike
To him who reigns, and so much to him due
Of hazard more, as he above the rest
High honour'd sits? Go, therefore, mighty powers,
Terror of heaven, though fallen; intend at home,
While here shall be our home, what best may ease
The present misery, and render hell
More tolerable; if there be cure or charm
To respite, or deceive, or slack the pain
Of this ill mansion: intermit no watch
Against a wakeful foe, while I abroad
Through all the coasts of dark destruction seek
Deliverance for us all: this enterprise
None shall partake but me.' Thus saying, rose
The monarch, and prevented all reply;
Prudent, lest, from his resolution raised
Others among the chief might offer now
(Certain to be refused) what erst they feared;
And, so refused, might in opinion stand
His rivals; winning cheap the high repute,
Which he through hazard huge must earn. But they
Dreaded not more the adventure, than his voice
Forbidding; and at once with him they rose:
Their rising all at once, was as the sound
Of thunder heard remote. Towards him they bend
With awful reverence prone: and as a god
Extol him equal to the Highest in heaven:
Nor fail'd they to express how much they praised,
That for the general safety he despised
His own: for neither do the spirits damn'd
Lose all their virtue; lest bad men should boast

Their specious deeds on earth which glory excites,
Or close ambition, varnish'd o'er with zeal.
Thus they their doubtful consultations dark
Ended, rejoicing in their matchless chief.
As when from mountain-tops the dusky clouds
Ascending, while the north wind sleeps, o'erspread
Heaven's cheerful face, the louring element
Scowls o'er the darken'd landskip snow, or shower;
If chance the radiant sun with farewell sweet
Extend his evening beam, the fields revive,
The birds their notes renew, and bleating herds
Attest their joy, that hill and valley rings.
O shame to men! devil with devil damn'd
Firm concord holds, men only disagree
Of creatures rational, though under hope
Of heavenly grace! and, God proclaiming peace,
Yet live in hatred, enmity, and strife,
Among themselves, and levy cruel wars,
Wasting the earth, each other to destroy;
As if (which might induce us to accord)
Man had not hellish foes enow besides,
That, day and night, for his destruction wait.
The Stygian council thus dissolved: and forth
In order came the grand infernal peers:
Midst came their mighty paramount, and seem'd
Alone the antagonist of heaven, nor less
Than hell's dread emperor, with pomp supreme,
And god-like imitated state: him round
A globe of fiery seraphim enclosed
With bright imblazonry, and horrent arms.
Then of their session ended they bid cry
With trumpets' regal sound the great result:
Toward the four winds four speedy cherubim
Put to their mouths the sounding alchymy,
By herald's voice explained; the hollow abyss
Heard far and wide, and all the host of hell
With deafening shout return'd them loud acclaim.
Thence more at ease their minds, and somewhat raised

By false presumptuous hope, the ranged powers
Disband, and wandering, each his several way
Pursues, as inclination or sad choice
Leads him perplex'd where he may likeliest find
Truce to his restless thoughts, and entertain
The irksome hours, till his great chief return.
Part on the plain, or in the air sublime,
Upon the wing, or in swift race contend,
As at the Olympian games or Pythian fields;
Part curb their fiery steeds, or shun the goal
With rapid wheels, or fronted brigades form.
As when to warn proud cities, war appears
Waged in the troubled sky, and armies rush
To battle in the clouds, before each van
Prick forth the aëry knights, and couch their spears,
Till thickest legions close; with feats of arms
From either end of heaven the welkin burns.
Others, with vast Typhœan rage more fell,
Rend up both rocks and hills, and ride the air
In whirlwind; hell scarce holds the wild uproar,
As when Alcides, from Œchalia crown'd
With conquest, felt the envenom'd robe, and tore
Through pain up by the roots Thessalian pines,
And Lichas from the top of Œta threw
Into the Euboic sea. Others more mild,
Retreated in a silent valley, sing
With notes angelical to many a harp
Their own heroic deeds, and hapless fall
By doom of battle; and complain that fate
Free virtue should inthral to force or chance.
Their song was partial; but the harmony
(What could it less when spirits immortal sing?)
Suspended hell, and took with ravishment
The thronging audience. In discourse more sweet
(For eloquence the soul, song charms the sense),
Others apart sat on a hill retired,
In thoughts more elevate, and reason'd high
Of providence, foreknowledge, will, and fate,

Fix'd fate, free will, foreknowledge absolute,
And found no end, in wandering mazes lost.
Of good and evil much they argued then,
Of happiness and final misery,
Passion and apathy, and glory and shame;
Vain wisdom all, and false philosophy:
Yet, with a pleasing sorcery could charm
Pain for a while, or anguish, and excite
Fallacious hope, or arm the obdured breast
With stubborn patience, as with triple steel.
Another part, in squadrons and gross bands,
On bold adventure to discover wide
That dismal world, if any clime perhaps
Might yield them easier habitation, bend
Four ways their flying march, along the banks
Of four infernal rivers, that disgorge
Into the burning lake their baleful streams:
Abhorred Styx, the flood of deadly hate;
Sad Acheron, of sorrow, black and deep;
Cocytus, named of lamentation loud
Heard on the rueful stream; fierce Phlegethon,
Whose waves of torrent fire inflame with rage.
Far off from these, a slow and silent stream,
Lethe, the river of oblivion, rolls
Her watery labyrinth, whereof who drinks,
Forthwith his former state and being forgets,
Forgets both joy and grief, pleasure and pain.
Beyond this flood a frozen continent
Lies dark and wild, beat with perpetual storms
Of whirlwind and dire hail, which on firm land
Thaws not, but gathers heap, and ruin seems
Of ancient pile: or else deep snow and ice,
A gulf profound as that Serbonian bog
Betwixt Damiata and mount Casius old,
Where armies whole have sunk: the parching air
Burns frore, and cold performs the effects of fire.
Thither by harpy-footed Furies haled,
At certain revolutions, all the damn'd

Are brought; and feel by turns the bitter change
Of fierce extremes, extremes by change more fierce:
From beds of raging fire, to starve in ice
Their soft ethereal warmth, and there to pine
Immoveable, infix'd, and frozen round,
Periods of time, thence hurried back to fire.
They ferry over this Lethean sound
Both to and fro, their sorrow to augment,
And wish and struggle, as they pass, to reach
The tempting stream, with one small drop to lose
In sweet forgetfulness all pain and woe,
All in one moment, and so near the brink;
But fate withstands, and to oppose the attempt
Medusa with Gorgonian terror guards
The ford, and of itself the water flies
All taste of living wight, as once it fled
The lip of Tantalus. Thus roving on
In confused march forlorn, the adventurous bands
With shuddering horror pale, and eyes aghast,
View'd first their lamentable lot, and found
No rest. Through many a dark and dreary vale
They pass'd, and many a region dolorous,
O'er many a frozen, many a fiery Alp,
Rocks, caves, lakes, fens, bogs, dens, and shades of death
A universe of death; which God by curse
Created evil, for evil only good;
Where all life dies, death lives, and nature breeds,
Perverse, all monstrous, all prodigious things,
Abominable, inutterable, and worse
Than fables yet have feign'd, or fear conceived,
Gorgons, and Hydras, and Chimeras dire.
Meanwhile, the adversary of God and man,
Satan, with thoughts inflamed of highest design,
Puts on swift wings, and toward the gates of hell
Explores his solitary flight: sometimes
He scours the right hand coast, sometimes the left;
Now shaves with level wing the deep, then soars
Up to the fiery concave towering high.

As when far off at sea a fleet descried
Hangs in the clouds, by equinoctial winds
Close sailing from Bengala, or the isles
Of Ternate and Tidore, whence merchants bring
Their spicy drugs; they, on the trading flood,
Through the wide Ethiopian to the Cape,
Ply stemming nightly toward the pole: so seem'd
Far off the flying fiend. At last appear
Hell bounds, high reaching to the horrid roof,
And thrice threefold the gates; three folds were brass,
Three iron, three of adamantine rock
Impenetrable, impaled with circling fire,
Yet unconsumed. Before the gates there sat
On either side a formidable shape;
The one seem'd woman to the waist, and fair;
But ended foul in many a scaly fold
Voluminous and vast; a serpent arm'd
With mortal sting; about her middle round
A cry of hell-hounds never-ceasing bark'd
With wide Cerberean mouths full loud, and rung
A hideous peal; yet, when they list, would creep,
If aught disturbed their noise, into her womb,
And kennel there; yet there still bask'd and howl'd
Within unseen. Far less abhorr'd than these
Vex'd Scylla, bathing in the sea that parts
Calabria from the hoarse Trinacrian shore;
Nor uglier follow the night-hag, when, call'd
In secret, riding through the air she comes,
Lured with the smell of infant blood, to dance
With Lapland witches, while the labouring moon
Eclipses at their charms. The other shape,
If shape it might be call'd that shape had none,
Distinguishable in member, joint, or limb;
Or substance might be call'd that shadow seem'd,
For each seem'd either; black it stood as night,
Fierce as ten Furies, terrible as hell,
And shook a dreadful dart; what seem'd his head,
The likeness of a kingly crown had on

Satan was now at hand, and from his seat
The monster moving onward came as fast
With horrid strides; hell trembled as he strode.
The undaunted fiend what this might be admired,
Admired, not fear'd; God and his Son except,
Created thing naught valued he, nor shunn'd;
And with disdainful look thus first began:
  'Whence, and what art thou, execrable shape,
That darest, though grim and terrible, advance
Thy miscreated front athwart my way
To yonder gates? Through them I mean to pass,
That be assured, without leave ask'd of thee:
Retire, or taste thy folly, and learn by proof,
Hell-born, not to contend with spirits of heaven.
  To whom the goblin full of wrath replied:
'Art thou that traitor-angel, art thou he,
Who first broke peace in heaven, and faith, till then
Unbroken; and in proud, rebellious arms,
Drew after him the third part of heaven's sons
Conjured against the Highest; for which both thou
And they, outcast from God, are here condemn'd
To waste eternal days in woe and pain?
And reckon'st thou thyself with spirits of heaven,
Hell-doomed, and breath'st defiance here and scorn,
Where I reign king, and to enrage thee more,
Thy king and lord? Back to thy punishment,
False fugitive, and to thy speed add wings,
Lest with a whip of scorpions I pursue
Thy lingering, or with one stroke of this dart
Strange horror seize thee, and pangs unfelt before.'
  So spake the grisly terror, and in shape,
So speaking and so threatening, grew tenfold
More dreadful and deform. On the other side,
Incensed with indignation, Satan stood
Unterrified, and like a comet burn'd,
That fires the length of Ophiuchus huge
In the Arctic sky, and from his horrid hair
Shakes pestilence and war. Each at the head

Levell'd his deadly aim: their fatal hands
No second stroke intend; and such a frown
Each cast at the other, as when two black clouds,
With heaven's artillery fraught, come rattling on
Over the Caspian, then stand front to front,
Hovering a space, till winds the signal blow
To join their dark encounter in mid air:
So frown'd the mighty combatants, that hell
Grew darker at their frown; so match'd they stood;
For never but once more was either like
To meet so great a foe: and now great deeds
Had been achieved, whereof all hell had rung,
Had not the snaky sorceress, that sat
Fast by hell-gate, and kept the fatal key,
Risen, and with hideous outcry rush'd between.
'O father, what intends thy hand,' she cried,
'Against thy only son? What fury, O son,
Possesses thee to bend that mortal dart
Against thy father's head? and know'st for whom?
For him who sits above and laughs the while
At thee ordain'd his drudge, to execute
Whate'er his wrath, which he calls justice, bids;
His wrath, which one day will destroy ye both.'
She spake, and at her words the hellish pest
Forebore; then these to her Satan return'd:
'So strange thy outcry, and thy words so strange,
Thou interposest, that my sudden hand,
Prevented, spares to tell thee yet by deeds
What it intends; till first I know of thee,
What thing thou art thus double-form'd; and why
In this infernal vale first met, thou call'st
Me father, and that phantasm call'st my son.
I know thee not, nor ever saw till now
Sight more detestable than him and thee.'
To whom thus the portress of hell-gate replied:
'Hast thou forgot me then, and do I seem
Now in thine eye so foul? once deem'd so fair
In heaven, when at the assembly, and in sight

Of all the seraphim with thee combined
In bold conspiracy against heaven's King,
All on a sudden miserable pain
Surprised thee, dim thine eyes, and dizzy swum
In darkness, while thy head flames thick and fast
Threw forth; till on the left side opening wide,
Likest to thee in shape and countenance bright,
Then shining heavenly fair, a goddess arm'd,
Out of thy head I sprung; amazement seized
All the host of heaven; back they recoil'd afraid
At first, and call'd me Sin, and for a sign
Portentous held me; but familiar grown,
I pleased, and with attractive graces won
The most averse, thee chiefly, who full oft
Thyself in me thy perfect image viewing,
Becamest enamour'd and such joy thou took'st
With me in secret, that my womb conceived
A growing burden. Meanwhile war arose,
And fields were fought in heaven; wherein remain'd
(For what could else?) to our Almighty Foe
Clear victory; to our part loss and rout,
Through all the empyréan: down they fell,
Driven headlong from the pitch of heaven, down
Into this deep; and in the general fall
I also: at which time this powerful key
Into my hand was given, with charge to keep
These gates for ever shut, which none can pass
Without my opening. Pensive here I sat
Alone; but long I sat not, till my womb,
Pregnant by thee, and now excessive grown,
Prodigious motion felt, and rueful throes.
At last this odious offspring whom thou seest,
Thine own begotten, breaking violent way,
Tore through my entrails, that, with fear and pain
Distorted, all my nether shape thus grew
Transform'd: but he my inbred enemy
Forth issued, brandishing his fatal dart
Made to destroy. I fled and cried out, Death!

Hell trembled at the hideous name, and sigh'd
From all her caves, and back resounded, Death!
I fled; but he pursued (though more, it seems,
Inflamed with lust than rage), and, swifter far
Me overtook his mother all dismay'd,
And in embraces forcible and foul
Ingendering with me, of that rape begot
These yelling monsters that with ceaseless cry
Surround me, as thou saw'st, hourly conceived
And hourly born, with sorrow infinite
To me; for when they list, into the womb
That bred them they return, and howl and gnaw
My bowels, their repast; then bursting forth
Afresh with conscious terrors vex me round,
That rest or intermission none I find.
Before mine eyes in opposition sits
Grim Death, my son and foe; who sets them on,
And me his parent would full soon devour
For want of other prey, but that he knows
His end with mine involved; and knows that I
Should prove a bitter morsel, and his bane,
Whenever that shall be; so fate pronounced.
But thou, O father, I forewarn thee, shun
His deadly arrow; neither vainly hope
To be invulnerable in those bright arms,
Though temper'd heavenly; for that mortal dint,
Save he who reigns above, none can resist.'
  She finished; and the subtle fiend his lore
Soon learn'd, now milder, and thus answer'd smooth:
  'Dear daughter, since thou claim'st me for thy sire,
And my fair son here show'st me, the dear pledge
Of dalliance had with thee in heaven, and joys
Then sweet, now sad to mention, through dire change
Befallen us, unforeseen, unthought of, know,
I come no enemy, but to set free
From out this dark and dismal house of pain
Both him and thee, and all the heavenly host
Of spirits, that, in our just pretences arm'd,

Fell with us from on high: from them I go
This uncouth errand sole; and one for all
Myself expose, with lonely steps to tread
The unsounded deep, and through the void immense
To search with wandering quest a place foretold
Should be, and, by concurring signs, ere now
Created vast and round, a place of bliss
In the purlieus of heaven, and therein placed
A race of upstart creatures, to supply
Perhaps our vacant room; though more removed,
Lest heaven, surcharged with potent multitude,
Might hap to move new broils. Be this or aught
Than this more secret now design'd, I haste
To know; and, this once known, shall soon return,
And bring ye to the place where thou and Death
Shall dwell at ease, and up and down unseen
Wing silently the buxom air embalm'd
With odours; there ye shall be fed and fill'd
Immeasurably; all things shall be your prey.'
He ceased, for both seem'd highly pleased, and Death
Grinn'd horrible a ghastly smile, to hear
His famine should be fill'd; and bless'd his maw
Destined to that good hour; no less rejoiced
His mother bad, and thus bespake her sire:
'The key of this infernal pit by due,
And by command of heaven's all-powerful King,
I keep, by him forbidden to unlock
These adamantine gates; against all force
Death ready stands to interpose his dart,
Fearless to be o'ermatch'd by living might.
But what owe I to his commands above
Who hates me, and hath hither thrust me down
Into this gloom of Tartarus profound,
To sit in hateful office here confined,
Inhabitant of heaven, and heavenly-born,
Here, in perpetual agony and pain,
With terrors and with clamours compass'd round
Of mine own brood, that on my bowels feed?

Thou art my father, thou my author, thou
My being gavest me; whom should I obey
But thee? whom follow? Thou wilt bring me soon
To that new world of light and bliss, among
The gods who live at ease, where I shall reign
At thy right hand voluptuous, as beseems
Thy daughter, and thy darling, without end.'
   Thus saying, from her side the fatal key,
Sad instrument of all our woe, she took;
And, towards the gate rolling her bestial train,
Forthwith the huge portcullis high up-drew,
Which, but herself, not all the Stygian powers
Could once have moved; then in the key-hole turns
The intricate wards, and every bolt and bar
Of massy iron or solid rock with ease
Unfastens. On a sudden open fly
With impetuous recoil and jarring sound
The infernal doors, and on their hinges grate
Harsh thunder, that the lowest bottom shook
Of Erebus. She open'd, but to shut
Excell'd her power; the gates wide open stood,
That with extended wings a banner'd host,
Under spread ensigns marching, might pass through
With horse and chariots rank'd in loose array;
So wide they stood, and like a furnace-mouth
Cast forth redounding smoke and ruddy flame.
Before their eyes in sudden view appear
The secrets of the hoary deep; a dark
Illimitable ocean without bound,
Without dimension, where length, breadth, and height,
And time, and place, are lost; where eldest Night
And Chaos, ancestors of Nature, hold
Eternal anarchy, amidst the noise
Of endless wars, and by confusion stand.
For Hot, Cold, Moist, and Dry, four champions fierce,
Strive here for mastery, and to battle bring
Their embryon atoms; they around the flag
Of each his faction, in their several clans,

Light-arm'd or heavy, sharp, smooth, swift, or slow,
Swarm populous, unnumber'd as the sands
Of Barca or Cyrene's torrid soil,
Levied to side with warring winds and poise,
Their lighter wings. To whom these most adhere,
He rules a moment: Chaos umpire sits,
And by decision more embroils the fray
By which he reigns: next him high arbiter
Chance governs all. Into this wild abyss,
The womb of Nature, and perhaps her grave,
Of neither sea, nor shore, nor air, nor fire,
But all these in their pregnant causes mix'd
Confus'dly, and which thus must ever fight,
Unless the Almighty Maker them ordain
His dark materials to create more worlds:
Into this wild abyss the wary fiend
Stood on the brink of hell, and look'd awhile,
Pondering his voyage; for no narrow frith
He had to cross. Nor was his ear less peal'd
With noises loud and ruinous (to compare
Great things with small), than when Bellona storms,
With all her battering engines bent to rase
Some capital city; or less than if this frame
Of heaven were falling, and these elements
In mutiny had from her axle torn
The stedfast earth. At last his sail-broad vans
He spreads for flight, and in the surging smoke
Uplifted spurns the ground; thence many a league,
As in a cloudy chair, ascending rides
Audacious; but, that seat soon failing, meets
A vast vacuity: all unawares
Fluttering his penons vain, plump down he drops
Ten thousand fathom deep; and to this hour
Down had been falling, had not by ill chance
The strong rebuff of some tumultuous cloud,
Instinct with fire and nitre, hurried him
As many miles aloft; that fury staid,
Quench'd in a boggy syrtis, neither sea,

Nor good dry land: nigh founder'd on he fares,
Treading the crude consistence, half on foot,
Half flying; behoves him now both oar and sail.
As when a gryphon through the wilderness
With winged course, o'er hill or moory dale,
Pursues the Arimaspian, who by stealth
Had from his wakeful custody purloin'd
The guarded gold: so eagerly the fiend
O'er bog, or steep, through straight, rough, dense, or rare,
With head, hands, wings, or feet, pursues his way,
And swims or sinks, or wades, or creeps, or flies.
At length, a universal hubbub wild
Of stunning sounds, and voices all confused,
Borne through the hollow dark, assaults his ear
With loudest vehemence; thither he plies,
Undaunted, to meet there whatever power
Or spirit of the nethermost abyss
Might in that noise reside, of whom to ask
Which way the nearest coast of darkness lies
Bordering on light; when straight behold the throne
Of Chaos, and his dark pavilion spread
Wide on the wasteful deep; with him enthroned,
Sat sable-vested Night, eldest of things,
The consort of his reign; and by them stood
Orcus and Ades, and the dreaded name
Of Demogorgon! Rumour next and Chance,
And Tumult and Confusion all embroil'd,
And Discord with a thousand various mouths.
To whom Satan turning boldly, thus: 'Ye powers
And spirits of this nethermost abyss,
Chaos and ancient Night, I come no spy,
With purpose to explore or to disturb
The secrets of your realm; but, by constraint
Wandering this darksome desert, as my way
Lies through your spacious empire up to light,
Alone, and without guide, half lost, I seek
What readiest path leads where your gloomy bounds

Confine with heaven; or if some other place,
From your dominion won, the ethereal King
Possesses lately, thither to arrive
I travel this profound; direct my course;
Directed no mean recompense it brings
To your behoof, if I that region lost,
All usurpation thence expell'd, reduce
To her original darkness, and your sway
(Which is my present journey), and once more
Erect the standard there of ancient Night:
Yours be the advantage all, mine the revenge.'
  Thus Satan; and him thus the Anarch old,
With faltering speech and visage incomposed,
Answer'd: 'I know thee stranger, who thou art,
That mighty leading angel, who of late
Made head against heaven's King, though overthrown.
I saw and heard; for such a numerous host
Fled not in silence through the frighted deep,
With ruin upon ruin, rout on rout,
Confusion worse confounded; and heaven-gate
Pour'd out by millions her victorious ban
Pursuing. I upon my frontiers here
Keep residence; if all I can will serve
That little which is left so to defend,
Encroach'd on still through your intestine broils
Weakening the sceptre of old Night: first hell,
Your dungeon, stretching far and wide beneath;
Now lately heaven and earth, another world,
Hung o'er my realm, link'd in a golden chain
To that side heaven from whence your legions fell:
If that way be your walk, you have not far;
So much the nearer danger; go, and speed,
Havoc, and spoil, and ruin, are my gain.'
  He ceased; and Satan stay'd not to reply,
But, glad that now his sea should find a shore,
With fresh alacrity, and force renew'd,
Springs upward like a pyramid of fire,

Into the wild expanse, and through the shock
Of fighting elements, on all sides round
Environ'd, wins his ways; harder beset
And more endanger'd, than when Argo pass'd
Through Bosporus, betwixt the jutting rocks:
Or when Ulysses on the larboard shunn'd
Charybdis, and by the other whirlpool steer'd,
So he with difficulty and labour hard
Moved on, with difficulty and labour he;
But, he once pass'd, soon after, when man fell,
Strange alteration! Sin and Death amain
Following his track, such was the will of Heaven,
Paved after him a broad and beaten way
Over the dark abyss, whose boiling gulf
Tamely endured a bridge of wondrous length,
From hell continued reaching the utmost orb
Of this frail world: by which the spirits perverse
With easy intercourse pass to and fro
To tempt or punish mortals, except whom
God and good angels guard by special grace.
But now at last the sacred influence
Of light appears, and from the walls of heaven
Shoots far into the bosom of dim Night,
A glimmering dawn: here nature first begins
Her farthest verge, and Chaos to retire,
As from her outmost works a broken foe,
With tumult less, and with less hostile din;
That Satan with less toil, and now with ease
Wafts on the calmer wave by dubious light,
And, like a weather-beaten vessel, holds
Gladly the port, though shrouds and tackle torn,
Or in the emptier waste, resembling air,
Weighs his spread wings, at leisure to behold
Far off the empyreal heaven, extended wide
In circuit, undetermined square or round,
With opal towers and battlements adorn'd
Of living sapphire, once his native seat:

And fast by, hanging in a golden chain,
This pendent world, in bigness as a star
Of smallest magnitude, close by the moon.
Thither, full fraught with mischievous revenge,
Accursed, and in a cursed hour, he hies

NOTES.

l. 2. Ormus or Hormuz is an island at the entrance of the Persian Gulf. In the early part of the sixteenth century the Portuguese took possession of it, and in their hands it became the emporium for the trade between India and Persia and Mesopotamia. The population of the chief town at that time amounted to 40,000. It was wrested from the Portuguese in 1622 by Shah Abbas the Great. The population at present is only between 300 and 400, who subsist by fishing and trading in salt, of which the island contains considerable quantities.

l. 3. Before *where* supply *of the region*. The clause *where—gold* is an adjective clause attached to *region* understood.

It is not necessary to repeat the entire sentence on account of the conjunction *or*, because, as thus used, it does not involve an *alternative*, but is pretty much the same in force as *and*. *Of Ormus*, *of Ind*, and *of* [*the region*] *where*, *&c.*, form attributive adjuncts of *wealth*. (*Gr.* 362, 4. *An.* 20, 4.)

l. 7. *From* is here equivalent to *just after*. Compare John xiii. 2, 4, "Supper being ended—he riseth from supper."

l. 8. *Beyond thus high* must be treated as an adverbial expression equivalent to *beyond this height*.

l. 12. The adverbial clause, *for I give not heaven for lost* (*Gr.* 423. *An.* 89), qualifies the predicate of a clause understood, *I call you deities of heaven*, or something of that kind. The adverbial clause *since no deep—vigor* qualifies *give*, and the adverbial clause *though* [*it be*] *oppressed and fallen* qualifies *can*.

l. 14. *From this descent*. Either *from* must be regarded as equivalent to *after*, as it is in *l.* 16, or else *descent* means *depth to which we have descended*.

l. 16. *Than, &c.* An elliptical adverbial clause qualifying *more.* In full, *than they would have appeared glorious and dread from no fall.* For a full explanation of the construction of all such clauses see *Gr.* 549—564. *An.* 151—172.

l. 17. *To fear, &c.* An adverbial adjunct of *trust* (*Gr.* 372, 2. *An.* 31, 2.)

l. 18. Take *me* as the object of *create* in *l.* 19. *Leader* forms the complement of the predicate *did create.* (*Gr.* 391. *An.* 50.)

l. 19. Before *next* repeat *though,* and after *merit* repeat *did create me your leader.* Both clauses are in the adverbial relation to *hath established.*

l. 21. *Of merit* forms an attributive adjunct to *what,* which is used here as a substantive pronoun, the subject of *hath been achieved.* (*Gr.* 362, 4. *An.* 20. 4. *Gr.* 147, 148.)

l. 23. After *established* repeat *me.*

l. 25. *In heaven,* an attributive adjunct of *state.*

l. 27. Before *whom* supply *him,* the object (understood) of *will envy.* (*Gr.* 148.)

l. 28. *Foremost* constitutes a complement of the predicate *exposes.* (*Gr.* 391. *An.* 50.) In like manner *bulwark* serves as complement to *stand.* Before *condemns* repeat *whom the highest place.*

l. 31. *For which* [*we need*] *to strive.* An elliptical adjective clause qualifying *good.*

l. 33. *None, &c.* In full, *for there is none in hell whose, &c.*

l. 34. *That, &c.* This clause is very awkward. Grammatically it is an adjective clause attached to *none, that* being a relative pronoun. But the sequence of ideas rather requires that we should have an adverbial clause beginning with the adverb *that,* and co-ordinate with the preceding adverb *so.* (*Gr.* 424, 528. *An.* 90, 133). In this case we should have to supply a subject *he.*

l. 36. *To union.* An attributive adjunct of *advantage.* (*Gr.* 362, 4. *An.* 20, 4.) [*To*] *firm faith,* and [*to*] *firm accord,* form similar adjuncts.

l. 37. *More* is an adjective qualifying *advantage.* It is itself qualified by the elliptical adverbial clause *than* [*it*] *can be* [*much*] *in heaven.* See *Gr.* 549, &c. *An.* 151, &c.

Surer to—us. An attributive adjunct of *we.* The adverbial clause *than prosperity could have assured us,* which qualifies the adjective *surer,* is not elliptical. *Assured* is equivalent to *made sure.*

l. 40. In full, *By what best way* [*we can claim our just inheritance of old*] *we now debate. Whether* [*we can claim our just inheritance by way*] *of open war, we now debate ; or* [*whether we can claim our just inheritance by way of*) *covert guile, we now debate.* The clauses beginning with *whether* are substantive clauses, objects of the verb *debate.* (*Gr.* 403, 406. *An.* 73, 76.) Before *who* apply *he.*

l. 43. The name *Molech* means *king* or *ruler.* Molech or Milcom was especially the national god of the Ammonites. To this god children were sacrificed by fire. The worship of Molech among the Israelites was at least as old as the time of Solomon (1 Kings xi. 7), if not older. Compare Jerem. vii. 31 ; Ezek. xvi. 21, xxiii. 37 ; 2 Kings xxiii. 13.

l. 46, &c. *To be deemed,* &c. Complement of the verb of incomplete predication *was.*

l. 47. *Than be less.* An elliptical adverbial clause attached to *rather,* the force of which it qualifies and explains. In full, *than* [*he would soon*] *be less.* See *Gr.* 560. *An.* 165.

l. 53. After *need* repeat *them.*

Or when, &c. In full : *Let those who need them contrive them when they need them ; let them not contrive them now.*

l. 54. *For shall the rest—sit,* &c. The interrogative clause *shall the rest,* &c. must be taken as the rhetorical equivalent of *the rest must not sit,* &c., or something of that kind. If this were substituted, we should get an adverbial clause which might be attached to the predicate *let* [*those*] *contrive.*

l. 57. Before *for* repeat *shall the rest.*

l. 59. *Who reigns,* &c., is an adjective clause attached to the *substantive* pronoun *his.* See *Gr.* 141.

l. 61. *Armed with hell flames and fury, all at once turning,* &c. It is not by any means so easy as it may seem at first sight, to assign a definite grammatical construction for *armed, all,* and *turning.* It is clear that they are not simple attributives of *us,* as they must be attached closely in sense to the infinitive mood *to force,* and that has no subject connected with it with which they might agree. We must look upon cases of this sort as instances of those anomalous constructions which are to be found in all languages, in which the connection of the ideas is more exact than the grammatical concatenation of the words. An infinitive mood retains a shade of the attributive nature of a verb ; hence it implies something of which it denotes an attribute, and so may be associated with other words whose attributive character is more strongly marked.

l. 64. *When to meet—thunder ;* [*when*] *for lightning* [*he shall*] *see* ——

angels, and [*when he shall see*] *his throne—torments*, are adverbial clauses of time attached to the participle *turning*. *To meet—engine*, forms an attributive adjunct of *thunder*. (*Gr.* 362, 4. *An.* 20, 4.) *For lightning* is an adverbial adjunct of the participle *shot*.

l. 71. *To scale*, &c. An adverbial adjunct of the adjectives *difficult* and *steep*. (Gr. 372, 2. *An.* 31, 2).

l. 72. *Upright wing* is a figurative expression for *upward flight*.

l. 73. Verbs like *bethink*, *remind*, &c., have a rather peculiar force. They are equivalent to *make think*, *make remember*, &c., and of the two objects which follow them, one is the object of the *make*, and the other of the complementary infinitive which follows. *Them* may be called the direct object of *bethink*, and the substantive clause *that—seat* the secondary object.

l. 73. *Sleepy drench*. An allusion to the Grecian fable of the effects of the stream *Lethe*.

Drench is a collateral form of *drink*. Compare *stench* and *stink*.

l. 75. Persons may still be met with who are not aware that those bodies which rise in water and air, do so, in fact, through the indirect action of forces which pull downwards. Such bodies do not *rise* up, they are *pushed* up.

l. 77. *Adverse*, that is, *contrary to our nature*.

Who but felt. For the explanation of this troublesome construction see (*Gr.* 522, compared with 502-505.)

l. 79. Before *pursued* repeat *when the fierce foe*.

l. 80. *With what—low*. A substantive clause, the object of *felt*, (*Gr.* 406. *An.* 76.)

l. 82. *Events*, i. e. *results*.

Should we—stronger is an adverbial clause of condition, attached to *may*. (*Gr.* 441. *An.* 93.)

l. 84. *To our destruction*. An attributive adjunct of *way*. (*Gr.* 362, 4. *An.* 20, 4.)

l. 85. *To be worse destroyed*. An attributive adjunct of *fear*.

l. 86. *Than to dwell here* [*is bad*]. An adverbial clause of *degree*, qualifying worse. (*Gr.* 549, &c. *An.* 151, &c.)

Driven, *condemned*. See note on *l.* 61.

l. 88. *Where pain—penance*. A compound adjective clause, attached to *deep*. (*Gr.* 408. *An.* 77.)

l. 90. *When the scourge*, &c. An adverbial clause of time, qualifying *exercise*. After *inexorable* supply *calls us to penance*.

l. 92. *Than thus:* that is, *than* [*we are*] *thus* [*destroyed*]. An elliptical adverbial clause of degree qualifying *more*.

l. 94. *What* (like *quid* in Latin) here means *why. Doubt* means *hesitate.*

l. 96. The construction of this sentence is inexact. The *or* in *l.* 99 should be followed by another verb in the infinitive, depending on *will.* As it stands, the sentence does not admit of strict analysis. To render it susceptible of this, we may substitute, *for either this, to the height enraged, will quite consume us,* &c.

l. 97. *Happier far,* &c. Here again the connection of the ideas is more obvious than the grammatical connection of the words. Before *happier* we may supply *a lot;* and to get anything that admits of being reduced to analytical rules, we must still further expand it into; *and this is a lot happier,* &c.

l. 98. *Than—being.* An elliptical adverbial clause. After *being* supply *is happy.* (Gr. 549, &c. *An.* 151, &c.)

Respecting the construction of *miserable,* see note on *l.* 61.

l. 102. *To disturb,* &c. and *to alarm,* &c., are adverbial adjuncts of *sufficient.* (*Gr.* 372, 2. *An.* 31, 2.)

l. 104. *Though* [*it is*] *inaccessible.* An elliptical adverbial clause, attached to *sufficient.*

l. 105. *Which,* &c. We cannot take this as an adjective clause attached to any particular preceding *substantive.* Treat *which* as equivalent to *and this.* After *if* supply *it be.*

l. 108. *To less than gods.* That is, *to beings less than gods are great.* (*Gr.* 549, &c. *An.* 151, &c.)

l. 111. *For dignity* and *for high exploit,* are adverbial adjuncts of *composed,* which is the complement of the verb of incomplete predication *seemed.* (*Gr.* 372, 2. *An.* 31, 2. *Gr.* 391. *An.* 50.)

l. 114. *To perplex,* &c. An adverbial adjunct of *make.*

l. 115. *For his thoughts—slothful.* An adverbial clause of cause attached to *was* in *l.* 112.

l. 120. *As* [*I am*] *not behind in hate.* An adverbial clause of cause attached to *should be.* (*Gr.* 288.)

What was urged, &c. An adjective clause used substantively, that is, qualifying a demonstrative understood, which, if expressed, would be the subject of *did dissuade.* (*Gr.* 148.)

l. 121. *Reason* forms a complement to the predicate *was urged.* (*Gr.* 391. *An.* 50.)

l. 123. *Success* :—that which *succeeds* or *comes after.*

l. 124. *When he—revenge.* A compound adverbial clause, attached to *did seem. Fact* is the same as *feat,* which is the form in which we have adopted the French *fait.*

l. 125. Analyse this as if it ran, *in that which he counsels and in that in which he excels.* We then get two complex adverbial adjuncts of *grounds.*

l. 127. After *as* we must supply *he would ground his courage on.* *Scope* means *that which is aimed at.*

l. 128. *After some dire revenge.* An attributive adjunct of *dissolution.* (*Gr.* 362, 4. *An.* 20, 4.)

l. 129. *First what revenge.* In full: *First I ask what revenge he would take.*

l. 130. *Access*: that is, *way of approach.*

l. 134. *Could we* is equivalent to *if we could.* Before *at* repeat *if.*

l. 142. *Thus repulsed.* Treat this as a nominative absolute, *we being thus repulsed.*

l. 146. *To be no more* is in apposition to *that,* to which accordingly it forms an attributive adjunct. (*Gr.* 362, 2. *An.* 20, 2.)

For who, &c. This adverbial clause qualifies the predicate of a clause understood. *I call it sad,* or something of that sort.

l. 149. *Swallowed,—lost,—devoid.* See note on *l.* 61.

l. 152. *Let this be good.* This is equivalent to the adverbial clause, *if we grant that this is good.*

l. 153. *Or will ever.* In full, *or who knows whether our angry foe will ever give it?*

l. 157. A contracted sentence. First leave out *or unaware*; then repeat the whole, substituting *unaware* for *through impotence.*

Impotence here means *want of self-control,* like the Latin *impotentia.*

l. 160. *We are decreed* [*to eternal woe*]; [*We are*] *reserved* [*to eternal woe*]; [*We are*] *destined to eternal woe; whatever doing, what can we suffer more; and* [*Whatever doing*], *what can we suffer worse,* are all quotations forming co-ordinate objects of *say.* (*Gr.* 397.)

l. 162. *Whatever doing.* This is not a strictly grammatical construction. It should be *whatever we do:* an adverbial clause of concession attached to *can.*

l. 164. Supply *we* with the participles, and *we being* with *in arms.* We then get three nominatives absolute, forming adverbial adjuncts to *is.*

l. 165. *What.* Supply *was the state of things,* or something of that kind.

Amain: with all our might. Connected with the Anglo-Saxon *magan, to be able.*

l. 168. Before *when* repeat *what was the state of things.*

l. 170. After *what* supply *will be our state.*

l. 172. Before *plunge* supply *if the breath that—fires, awaked, should.* After *or* supply *what will be our case. From above* is an adverbial adjunct of *should arm. Should vengeance arm,* is of course the same as *if vengeance should arm.*

l. 174. *What.* See note on *l.* 170.

l. 175. Before *this* repeat *if.*

l. 178. *While we—hopeless end.* A compound adverbial clause of time, attached to *should spout.*

l. 179. First leave out *or exhorting:* then repeat the whole clause *while we—whirlwinds,* substituting *exhorting* for *designing.*

l. 182. After *or* repeat *while we perhaps designing or exhorting glorious war, caught in a fiery tempest shall be;* then subdivide the clause into two in the same way as the last.

l. 181. Compare Virgil *Æn.* i. 44, 45, where he describes the fate of Ajax, the son of Oileus :—

> Illum expirantem transfixo pectore flammas
> Turbine corripuit, scopuloque infixit acuto.

The *sport,* &c. Compare Virgil *Æn.* vi. 740. Aliæ panduntur inanes suspensæ ad ventos.

Wracking is not the same as *racking,* but is a collateral form of *wrecking.*

l. 185. This repetition of a negative adjective is very common in poetry. Thus in book iii. 231, we have *unprevented, unimplored, unsought.* In Shakspere (*Hamlet, Act I.*), *unhousel'd, unappointed, unannealed.*

l. 186. *Ages of hopeless end.* That is, *ages, the end of which is not to be hoped for.*

l. 187. Subdivide this sentence as follows :—*War therefore, open, my voice dissuades, for what can force with him. War therefore, concealed, my voice dissuades, for what can guile with him. War therefore, concealed, my voice dissuades, for who can deceive his mind—view.*

l. 191. First leave out *and derides,* then repeat the whole sentence *He from Heaven's height—wills,* substituting *derides* for *sees.* Compare *Psalm* ii. 4.—"He that sitteth in the heaven shall laugh; the Lord shall have them in derision."

l. 193. After *than* supply *he is.* An adverbial clause of degree qualifying and defining *more.* (*Gr.* 549, &c. *An.* 151.)

To resist, &c., is an adverbial adjunct of *almighty,* and *to frustrate,* &c. of *wise.* (*Gr.* 372, 2. *An.* 31, 2.)

l. 194. *Vile* forms the complement of *hire*. (*Gr.* 391. *An.* 50.)

l. 196. In full, *these* [*are*] *better than worse* [*are good*.]

l. 198. In full, *and* [*since*] *omnipotent decree, the victor's will* [*subdues us*].

l. 199. *To suffer*, &c. This construction is very harsh. Analyse it as if it were, *our strength is as great to suffer as* [*it is great*] *to do*.

l. 200. Substitute (for analysis): *And the law is not unjust*, &c.

l. 201. *This was at first resolved*. That is, *this would have been at first resolved*. Milton imitates the common Latin construction, in which in hypothetical sentences, the verb of the consequent clause is in the indicative mood, although that of the hypothetical clause is in the subjunctive, in order to mark the assumed certainty of the consequence. Thus Cicero, *Mil.* 11. Quod si ita putasset, certe optabilius Miloni fuit dare jugulum. And 22. Quos nisi manumisisset, tormentis etiam dedendi fuerunt. See Zumpt. *Lat. Gr.* 519.

l. 203. Verbs take objects after them not because they are *verbs*, but because they denote an action or feeling directed to some object. For a similar reason many adjectives take objects after them, at least in the shape of substantive clauses.

l. 205. Before *fear* repeat *when those who—fail them*.

l. 206. *To endure exile, to endure ignominy*, &c., are phrases in apposition to *what they yet know must follow*. (See *Gr.* 362, 2. *An.* 20, 2.)

l. 209. *Which if we can sustain and bear*, is simply equivalent to *and if we can sustain and bear this*. It should not be taken as an adjective clause attached to *doom*, because the relative belongs to the hypothetical (adverbial) clause introduced by *if*, which is attached to the verb *may remit*.

l. 211. *And perhaps* [*our supreme foe*] *may not mind*, &c. After *perhaps* repeat *if we can sustain and bear this*.

l. 213. *With what is punished*; that is, *with the punishment that has been inflicted*. This is an imitation of the Latin neuter passive, but it is not good English.

l. 213. For *whence* substitute *and hence*. See *l.* 209.

l. 216. In full. *Our purer essence, inured, will not feel their noxious vapour*.

l. 219. *Familiar* and *void* qualify the subject of the sentence *essence*, which must be repeated.

l. 221. *What hope*. Analyse as if it were *that hope which*.

l. 222. In full. *Besides that chance which the never-ending flight of future days may bring, besides that change worth waiting which—bring*

We thus get three prepositional phrases (*Gr.* 372, 2. *An.* 31, 2.) forming adverbial adjuncts, but their connection with what precedes is very loose. They are connected with its general sense, rather than with any particular verb.

l. 223. *Waiting.* *Awaiting* would be more accurate.

Since—more woe. A compound adverbial sentence, qualifying *worth.* The natural order of the words is somewhat inverted. *Since our present lot appears for ill, not worst, though for happy it is but ill. For ill* is an adverbial adjunct of *worst,* and *for happy* of *ill.* *If we—woe* is an adverbial clause attached to *appears.*

l. 228. In full. *He did not counsel peace.*

l. 230. Before *to regain* repeat *we war.*

l. 234. *To hope.* An adverbial adjunct of *vain.* (*Gr.* 372, 2. *An.* 31, 2.) *As* is used in the sense of *equally.* The adjective *vain,* which it qualifies, forms the complement of the predicate *argues.* (*Gr.* 391. *An.* 50.)

l. 235. *For what,* &c. An adverbial clause attached to *argues.*

l. 236. *Unless—overpower.* An adverbial clause attached to *can be.*

l. 237. [*That*] *he should relent.* A substantive clause, the object of *suppose.*

Although grammatically the clause *suppose—subjection* is not connected with what follows, yet the relation of ideas is the same as though it began with *if* instead of *suppose,* and so formed an adverbial clause, attached to *could stand* and *could receive.*

l. 240. Before *receive* repeat *with what eyes could we.*

l. 241. *To celebrate,* &c., and to *sing,* &c., form attributive adjuncts of *laws.* (*Gr.* 362, 4. *An.* 20, 4.)

l. 243. *While—sovran,* and [*while*] *his altar—offerings,* are adverbial clauses which must be taken with each of the preceding predicates *could stand* and *could receive.*

l. 244. *Sovran* is the proper mode of spelling this word. (*Ital. sovrano.*) The spelling *sovereign* has been introduced through a blundering notion that the word was connected with *reign.*

Breathes. In this sense we are more familiar with the Latin word *exhale.*

l. 248. *In worship,* &c. An adverbial adjunct of *spent.*

l. 249. *Whom we hate.* An adjective clause, qualifying *him* understood.

l. 250. *By force.* An adverbial adjunct of *impossible.* *By leave obtained,* an adverbial adjunct of *unacceptable.* Both the adjectives qualify the object *state.*

l. 251. *Though* [*it be*] *in heaven.* An adverbial clause attached to the adjective *unacceptable.*

l. 254. *Though* [*we live*] *in the vast recess.* An adverbial clause attached to the predicate *let.* *Free* and *accountable* qualify *us* understood in *l.* 253.

l. 258. In full: "When [we can create] great things of small [things], [when we can create] useful [things] of hurtful [things]; [when we can create] prosperous [things] of adverse [things], and [when], in what place soever [we be, we can] thrive under evil, and [when in whatsoever place we be we can] work ease out of pain through labour and endurance."

l. 265. *His glory unobscured.* A nominative absolute, forming an adverbial adjunct to *reside.*

l. 266. Before *with* repeat *how oft heaven's all-ruling Sire.*

l. 267. *From whence—hell.* An adjective clause, qualifying *darkness.* Compare Psalm xviii. 11; xcvii. 2; Revelation iv. 5.

l. 268. *And heaven resembles hell.* This clause is but loosely attached to what precedes. Strictly it ought to be co-ordinate with *from whence—rage;* but we get very little sense by the insertion of *from whence.* It had better be taken as an independent sentence.

l. 269. *As he* [*imitates*] *our darkness.* An adverbial clause of manner qualifying *imitate.*

l. 272. *Nor want—magnificence.* First leave out *or art,* and then repeat the whole, substituting *art* for *skill.*

l. 275. In full: *these piercing fires may become as soft as they are now severe.* *As they are now severe* is an adverbial clause of degree qualifying the *as* which qualifies *soft.*

l. 276. *Our temper changed.* A nominative absolute, forming an adverbial adjunct to the predicate of each of the two last sentences.

l. 277. *Which,* &c. See note on *l.* 105.

l. 278. *The sensible of pain:*—so much of pain as is sensible, or may be felt.

l. 279. After *and* repeat *to.*

l. 280. *How in safety—of war.* A verb takes an object after it, because it denotes an action directed towards some object. But adjectives, and even nouns, may have a similar force. See note on *l.* 203. Here the substantive clause *How,* &c., forms a sort of object to *counsel.*

l. 282. *And where.* That is, *and with regard of the place where we are.* *With regard,* &c., forms an adverbial adjunct of *compose.* *What we are* is an adjective clause qualifying *that* understood. See *Gr.* 148. *What* is the complement of the predicate *are.* (*Gr.* 193, 4a. 99.)

l. 283. *What I advise.* An adjective clause used substantively, that is (in fact), qualifying *that* understood.

l. 284. The adverbial clause beginning with *when* goes on to *tempest.*

l. 285. *As when,* &c. That is, *as* [*the murmur is which is heard*] *when,* &c. This adverbial clause goes down to *tempest* and qualifies *such.*

l. 287. Before *now* repeat *which.*

l. 288. *Whose bark,* &c. A compound adjective clause qualifying *men.* First leave out *or pinnace,* and then repeat the whole, substituting *pinnace* for *bark.*

Compare Virgil *Æn.* x. 96.

Cunctique fremebant
Cœlicolæ assensu vario; ceu flamina prima,
Cum deprensa fremunt silvis, et cœca volutant
Murmura, venturos nautis prodentia ventos.

l. 293. *Than hell.* In full : *than they dreaded hell much.* (*Gr.* 549, &c. *An.* 151, &c.)

l. 296. *To found—heaven.* A complex attributive adjunct of *desire.* (*Gr.* 362, 4. *An.* 20, 4).

l. 299. *Which,* &c. That is, *and when Beëlzebub perceived this.* (See note on *l.* 105, 277.)

l. 299. *Beëlzebub.* The proper spelling of this word, where it occurs in the New Testament, is *Beëlzebul.* The people of Edom worshipped Baäl under the name of *Baal-zebub,* or the Lord of Flies,* just as in Elis sacrifices were offered to *Zeus apomyios,* or *Zeus, the averter of flies.* (Pausan. v. 14, 1.) By way of expressing contempt for idolatrous practices, the Jews in later times altered this name into Baalzebul, or Beëlzebul, which means the *Lord of dung,* and this name seems to have been applied as an epithet to Satan, unless we are to suppose, as some commentators do, that the Jews considered Beëlzebul as a separate personage, the leader or chief of the *demons* so frequently mentioned by the evangelists. (See *Matthew* xii. 24, &c. *Luke* xi. 15, &c.

Than whom. There is no grammatical principle on which this objective case can be defended. Relative pronouns ought to obey the same laws of construction as personal or demonstrative pronouns. With a personal pronoun the sentence would be, *none sat higher than he* [*sat high*].

l. 300. *Satan except,* equivalent to *Satan excepted,* a nominative absolute, forming an adverbial adjunct to the predicate. With this description compare Homer *Il.* iii. 216.

* 2 Kings i. 2.

l. 302. *A pillar of state.* Compare *Galat.* ii. 9. "When James, Cephas, and John, who seemed to be pillars, &c. Shakspere, 2 Henry VI., Act i. "Brave peers of England, pillars of the state."

l. 305. *Majestic*, qualified by the elliptical adverbial clause *though* [*it was*] *in ruin*, forms the complement of the predicate shone. (*Gr.* 391. *An.* 50.)

l. 308. *As night*, &c. In full: *As night is still, or as summer's noontide air is still.* Two adverbial clauses qualifying *still.*

l. 311. *Or*, &c. There can be no legitimate grammatical co-ordination between a vocative, or nominative of appellation, and an interrogative sentence.

l. 312. Before *be called* repeat *must we.*

l. 313. *For so*, &c. This complicated adverbial clause goes on to the end of *l.* 328. It is attached to the predicate *must* in each of the preceding sentences.

l. 314. *To continue* and *to build up*, &c., may be taken as adverbial adjuncts of *inclines.* (*Gr.* 372, 2. *An.* 31, 2.)

l. 316. Before *know* repeat *while we.*

l. 317. *Dungeon* forms a complement to the predicate *dooms.* (*Gr.* 391. *An.* 50.)

Not our safe, &c. In full: *And while we know not that the King of heaven hath not doomed this place our safe retreat*, &c. These adverbial clauses beginning with *while* are attached to the predicate *inclines.*.

l. 318. *To live*, &c. An adverbial adjunct of *hath doomed*. *Exempt.* See note on *l.* 61.

l. 320. *Banded.* See note on *l.* 61. *To remain—multitude.* A complex adverbial adjunct attached to *hath doomed.* The nucleus of it consists of an infinitive mood preceded by a preposition. (*Gr.* 372, 2. *An.* 31, 2.)

l. 321. *Though* [*we are*] *thus far removed.* An adverbial clause qualifying the predicate *hath doomed.* Respecting *reserved*, see note on *l.* 61.

l. 323. *For he—heaven.* This compound adverbial clause had better be attached to *hath doomed* in *l.* 316. *Be sure* must be taken as a separate parenthetical clause.

l. 324. First leave out *or depth*, and then repeat the whole clause *for he—heaven*, substituting *depth* for *height.*

l. 328. *As with his golden* [*sceptre he rules*] *those in heaven.* An adverbial clause of manner, attached to *will rule.*

l. 329. *What* is here an adverb, equivalent to *why*. See *l.* 94.

l. 331. In full: *Terms of peace yet none have been vouchsafed, or terms of peace yet none have been sought.* The clause *for what peace will be—inflicted,* must be attached to the predicate *have been vouchsafed,* and the clause *for what peace can we—suffering feel* to the predicate *hath been sought.* *But custody, but stripes,* and *but punishment,* form adverbial adjuncts of *will be given.* (*Gr.* 372, 2. *An.* 31, 2.) *But* is here a preposition. (*Gr.* 282, note.)

l. 336. *To our power* is an attributive adjunct of *hostility* and *hate.* *But hostility, but hate, but reluctance,* and *but revenge* form adverbial adjuncts of *can.* *Though* [*it be*] *slow* is an adverbial clause attached to *plotting.*

l. 341. *Want,* that is, *be wanting.* See Book I. 715.

l. 343. *Assault, siege,* and *ambush,* are co-ordinate objects of *fear.* The conjunction *or* here does not involve an *alternative.*

l. 344. After *what* supply *shall we say,* or something of that kind.

l. 349. *To be created,* &c. An attributive adjunct of *race.* *Though he be less in power and excellence* is an adverbial clause qualifying *favoured.*

l. 350. *But* is here superfluous.

l. 355. *What creatures there inhabit, of what mould they are; of what substance they are; how endued they are; what their power is; where their weakness is; how they may be attempted best; if they may be attempted best by force; or if they may be attempted best by subtlety,* form a series of substantive (interrogative) clauses, the objects of *learn.*

l. 365. *To waste,* &c., forms the subject of a predicate *may be achieved,* understood. Supply the same predicate with each of the infinitives that follow.

l. 367. *If* [*we can*] *not drive.* An adverbial clause attached to the predicate *may be achieved* that has to be supplied for the subject *to seduce,* &c. The adverbial clauses *that their God—foe,* and *that their God with repenting hand may abolish his own works,* are attached to the same predicate.

l. 373. The adverbial clause *when his darling—soon* should be repeated with each of the predicates *would surpass, would interrupt,* and *would upraise.*

l. 377. In full: *if to sit in darkness here, hatching vain empires, be better.* When *if* is equivalent to *whether* it introduces a substantive clause.

l. 380. *For whence—Creator.* This adverbial clause should be attached to the predicate of a sentence that must be supplied;—*I say first devised by Satan.* The interrogative form *whence* &c. is used as the rhetorical equivalent of *from no source,* &c.

l. 382. *To confound,* &c., and *to mingle and involve,* &c., form attributive adjuncts of *malice.* (*Gr.* 362, 4. *An.* 20, 4.)

l. 390. Repeat *have ye* before *ended* and *resolved.*

l. 394. *Perhaps,* &c. In full: *which will perhaps lift us up to a place in view,* &c.

l. 395. *Whence—heaven.* An adjective clause qualifying *place* understood.

l. 397. *Or else,* &c. The grammatical connection of the clause requires us to repeat *whence we may,* but though the general sense is plain enough, the sentence is very harshly constructed. We must suppose it equivalent to *whence we may make our way into some mild zone, and there dwell,* &c.

l. 407. *Uncouth* means *unknown.* In Anglo-Saxon *uncuð,* from *cunnan.* (*Gr. Addenda.*)

l. 409. *Arrive,* in the sense of *reach,* is also used by Shakspere, *Julius Cæsar,* Act I. Sc. 2:

"But ere we could arrive the point proposed."

l. 411. *Evasion* literally means, *making one's way out.*

l. 413. The omission of the preposition *of* after the noun *need* is very harsh, and in fact ungrammatical. It would be equally improper to take *had need* as equivalent to *would need.*

l. 415. Supply the antecedent *him* before *whom.*

l. 417. *This said.* A nominative absolute, forming an adverbial adjunct to *sat.*

l. 418. *Suspense* forms the complement to the predicate *held.* (*Gr.* 391. *An.* 50.) *Suspense* is here used quite legitimately as an adjective, though it has since come to be used only as a substantive. *Who appeared to second the perilous attempt; who appeared to oppose* &c., *who appeared to undertake the* &c., are three substantive clauses (*Gr.* 406. *An.* 76), in the objective relation to *awaiting.*

l. 425. *Hardy* forms the complement of the predicate *could be found.* *As to proffer,* &c. In full: *as* [*he would be hardy*] *to proffer* [*alone the dreadful voyage*], *or* [*as he would be hardy to*] *accept alone the dreadful voyage.* Two adverbial clauses qualifying the *so,* which qualifies *hardy.* *To proffer,* &c., and *to accept,* &c., form adverbial adjuncts of *hardy,* understood. (*Gr.* 372, 2. *An.* 31, 2.)

l. 426. *Till at last,* &c. An adverbial clause of time, attached to the predicate *could be found.*

l. 430. *Empyreal.* Derived from the Greek *en* (in), and *pyr* (fire).

Several of the ancient Greek and Roman philosophers held that the ultimate principle of all things is *fire*, and that other material substances,—air, water, earth,—consist of this primary principle in various stages of condensation into grosser forms, and in turn admit of being again rarefied into this primal element, the region of which is beyond that of the air, in proximity to the sun and the other heavenly bodies. This doctrine was propounded by Heraclitus, and was adopted by the Stoics. Hence, *empyreal* means *situated in the region of fire*, that is, in the *sky*, or *heaven*.

l. 432. *Though* [*we are*] *undismayed.* An adverbial clause of condition, attached to *hath seized.*

Long is the way, &c. Compare Virgil, *Æn.* VI. 128:—

> "Sed revocare gradum, superasque evadere ad auras,
> Hoc opus, hic labor est."

l. 436. *Ninefold.* So Virgil (*Æn.* VI. 439) says,—

> "Novies Styx interfusa coercet."

Adamant is anything excessively hard. The Greeks usually meant *steel* by it. It is the origin of the word *diamond.*

l. 438. *There passed.* A nominative absolute, forming an adverbial adjunct to *receives. If any pass* [*them*] is an adverbial clause, qualifying the participle *passed.*

l. 442. *Into whatever world.* In full: *into any world, whatever world it may be*, where *whatever*, &c., constitutes an adverbial clause attached to *escape;* and *whatever* is the complement of the predicate *may be* understood. (*Gr.* 530. *An.* 140. *Gr.* 495, 509. *An.* 99, 118.)

l. 444. *Than unknown dangers* [*are great*] *and* [*than*] *as* (i. e. *equally*) *hard escape* [*is great*]. Two adverbial clauses of degree attached to *less.* (*Gr.* 549, &c. *An.* 151, &c.)

l. 448. *In the shape*, &c. An attributive adjunct of *aught.* (*Gr.* 362, 4. *An.* 20, 4.)

l. 450. *From attempting.* An adverbial adjunct of *deter.*

Wherefore, &c. A very involved and awkward sentence. There are two principal co-ordinate sentences, *Wherefore do I assume these royalties, refusing to accept*, &c.; and *Wherefore do I not refuse to reign, refusing to accept*, &c.

l. 453. *As of honour.* An elliptical adverbial clause, co-ordinate with the demonstrative *as*, which qualifies *great.* In full: *as* [*I accept a great share*] *of honour.* (*Gr.* 548, &c., and note, p. 166, 15th ed. *An.* p. 42.) The second *as* is a connective or relative adverb, and qualifies *great* understood, just as the first *as* qualifies *great* expressed. (*Gr.* 422, 548.)

Due, &c. This adjective has no proper grammatical connection with what precedes. It relates both to *hazard* and to *honour*.

l. 454. *And so much*, &c. These words cannot be brought within the domain of any ordinary laws of Syntax. If we were to leave out *and* and insert *being*,--*so much more of hazard being due to him*,—we might treat this as a nominative absolute, forming an adverbial adjunct, attached to *due* in *l.* 453.

l. 455. *As he—sits*. An adverbial clause co-ordinate with *so*. *As* is in the adverbial relation to *high*. (*Gr.* 422, 548.)

l. 457. *Though* [*ye are*] *fallen*. This adverbial clause is attached to the noun *terror*, which is here used as an attributive adjunct. *Intend* means here *consider attentively*.

l. 458. The clauses beginning with *what* and *if* (in the sense of *whether*) are substantive clauses in the objective relation to *intend*.

l. 460. *If there be*, &c. This compound sentence is contracted. In full it is: *Intend at home if there be cure to respite the pain of this ill mansion. Intend at home if there be charm to respite the pain of this ill mansion.* Then repeat both these sentences with *deceive* instead of *respite*; and again with *slack* instead of *deceive*.

l. 467. Before *prevented* repeat *thus saying the monarch*. The attributive adjunct *prudent*, with all that belongs to it, must be attached to the subject in each sentence.

l. 468. *Prudent* here means *being on his guard*. The compound adverbial clause *lest—must earn* had better be attached to *prudent*. It might also be connected with the predicate *prevented*.

l. 469. *Among the chief* forms an attributive adjunct of *others*.

l. 470. *What erst they feared*. An adjective clause used substantively, *i. e.*, in fact, qualifying a demonstrative *that*, understood. (*Gr.* 148.)

Erst is the superlative answering to the old comparative *ere*, meaning *sooner*.

l. 471. Before *so* repeat *lest others*.

Rivals forms a complement to the predicate *stand*. (*Gr.* 391. *An.* 50.)

l. 474. *Than*, &c. In full: *than* [*they dreaded much*] *his voice forbidding*. An adverbial clause of degree, qualifying more.

l. 476. The adverbial clause *as* [*is*] *the sound—remote*, qualifies *was*.

l. 479. *Equal* forms a complement to the predicate *extol*. *As a god*: in full,—*as* [*they would extol*] *a god*.

l. 481. *That for—his own* [*safety*]. A substantive clause, the object of *praised*. The entire clause, *how much—his own*, is the object of *express*.

l. 482. *For neither—zeal.* A complex adverbial sentence attached to *failed.* The secondary adverbial clause, *lest bad—zeal*, qualifies *lose.*

l. 485. Before *close* repeat *which*, and after *zeal* repeat *excites.* *Close* here means *crafty.* It is a translation of the Greek *pyknos.*

l. 488. The connective adverb *as* qualifies the verbs *revive, renew,* and *attest.* The entire compound clause *as when—rings* is in the adverbial relation to *rejoicing.* It must be separated into three distinct clauses, *as the fields revive, as the birds their notes renew,* and *as the bleating herds attest their joy*, to the predicate of each of which must be attached the adverbial clauses *when from—face,* [*when*] *the lowering—snow,* [*when the lowering elements scowl o'er the darkened landscape*] *shower*, and *if chance the radiant—beam;* and the adverbial clause *that hill and valley rings*, must, in addition, be attached to the predicates *renew* and *attest.*

l. 498. *Though* [*they are*] *under—grace.* An elliptical adverbial clause qualifying *disagree.*

l. 499. *God proclaiming peace.* A nominative absolute, forming an adverbial adjunct to *live* and *levy.*

l. 503. *As if*, &c. An elliptical clause. In full: *as* [*they would waste the earth*] *if*, &c. The subordinate compound adverbial clause, *if—wait*, qualifies the verb *waste* understood.

l. 508. Before *seemed* repeat *their mighty paramount.* *Antagonist* forms the complement of *seemed.* (*Gr.* 391. *An.* 50.)

l. 509. *Nor less*, &c. That is, *and* [*their mighty paramount seemed*] *not less than hell's dread emperor* [*is great*] *with pomp supreme and* [*with*] *god-like imitated state.*

l. 513. *Horrent.* That is, *bristling.*

l. 517. *Alchemy.* In Milton's days *alchemy*, or chemistry, busied itself chiefly with the attempt to transmute the baser metals into gold. Alchemy is here used by a bold (not to say harsh) figure of speech, for some metal, the result of alchemy. Critics say that this is very poetical.

l. 518. *Explained.* That is, the meaning or purpose of the blast of the trumpets is explained by a herald.

l. 521. In full: *their minds being more at ease, and their minds being somewhat raised by false presumptuous hope.* Two nominatives absolute, forming adverbial adjuncts to *disband* and *pursues.*

l. 524. *As inclination*, &c. Separate into two adverbial clauses, *as inclination leads him, or as sad choice leads him*, and to the object *him* in each clause attach *perplexed*, with all that belongs to it. *Perplexed* must be taken as equivalent to *considering in perplexity.*

Then the clauses *where he may likeliest find*, &c., and *where he may likeliest entertain*, &c., form substantive clauses, the objects of *considering*.

l. 528. The parts of this sentence should be thus pieced together: *part on the plain in swift race contend, part in the air sublime upon the wing contend.* Then *both* these sentences must be repeated with *each* of the adverbial clauses, *as* [*men contended*] *at the Olympian games*, and [*as men contended*] *at the Pythian fields*. Compare Virgil, *Æn.* VI. 642:—

"Pars in gramineis exercent membra palæstris,
Contendunt ludo, et fulva luctantur arena:
Pars pedibus plaudunt choreas, et carmina dicunt," &c.

The four great national games of the Greeks were the Olympia, celebrated every four years in the plain of Olympia in Elis, in honour of Zeus; the Pythia, celebrated at first every eight years, but afterwards, every four years, near Delphi (anciently called Pytho), in honour of Apollo, Artemis, and Leto, at first under the management of the Delphians, afterwards under that of the Amphictyons; the Isthmia were held at the isthmus of Corinth, in honour of Poseidon, twice in every Olympiad, under the presidency of the Corinthians; the Nemea were held twice in each Olympiad, at Nemea in Argolis, in honour of Zeus. For the details of these solemnities the reader had better consult *Smith's Dictionary of Greek and Roman Antiquities*.

l. 531. Compare Horace, *Od.* I. 1, 4:—

"Metaque fervidis
Evitata rotis."

l. 532. *Fronted*, i. e., standing face to face.

l. 533. *As when—burns.* A compound elliptical adverbial clause, attached to *form*. After *as* supply *opposing forces meet*, or something of that kind; to the predicate of which the clause *when—burns* must be attached. This last clause is compound. Supply *when* before *armies* and *before*, and *when the aery knights* before *couch*. Repeat *when* before *with feats of arms*.

l. 538. *Welkin* is the *cloud-covered sky*. It is connected with the German *Wolken*, 'clouds.' *Burns* is here used in the same sense as *fervere* in Virgil, *Georg.* I. 456:—

"Omnia vento nimbisque videbis fervere."

l. 539. *Typhœan*. See Book I. 199.

l. 542. *As when*, &c. The grammatical connection of this with what precedes is very slight. Some clause must be supplied after *as* (such as *rocks and trees were rent up*), to the predicate of which the clause *when—sea* may be attached. It would make the sentence simpler if we omitted *when* before *Alcides*, and inserted it before *from*, putting in *he* before *felt*, and omitting *and* before *tore*. As the sentence stands in the text we must repeat *when Alcides* before *tore*, and before Lichas.

Alcides, &c. Hercules was so called because his mother Alcmena was the wife of Amphitryon, the son of Alcæus. But Hercules claimed Zeus as his father. Eurytus, king of Œchalia (a town either of Eubœa or of Thessaly), had promised his daughter Iole to any one who conquered him in archery, but refused to surrender her to Hercules, when the latter had won her. Hercules attacked Œchalia, slew Eurytus and his sons, and carried off Iole. When about to offer a sacrifice to celebrate his victory, he sent his attendant, Lichas, for a white robe from home. His wife, Dejanira, imbued this robe with a preparation of the blood of the centaur Nessus, whom Hercules had shot with a poisoned arrow, when he was attempting to carry Dejanira off, and who directed her to use his blood as a philtre, to preserve the love of her husband. The venom with which the robe was imbued soon attacked the body of Hercules, and occasioned him such agony that in his frenzy he hurled Lichas into the sea. Being unable to get rid of the robe, he erected a pile of wood, on which he caused himself to be burnt to death.

l. 550. *By doom of battle* forms an attributive adjunct to *fall*.

l. 551. Before *chance* repeat, *others complain that fate should enthrall free virtue to.*

l. 556. *For eloquence*, &c. This adverbial clause must be attached to the predicate of a sentence understood, *I call it more sweet*, or something of that kind. The whole is parenthetical, and does not enter into the construction of the main sentence.

l. 558. Before *reasoned* supply *they* or *others*.

l. 559. *Of providence.* Repeat the preposition before each of the nouns that follow. We thus get a series of adverbial adjuncts to *reasoned*.

l. 565. *Vain wisdom all.* The verb *was* must be supplied in order to make a combination that admits of analysis.

l. 566. Before *could* supply *this*.

l. 567. Before *anguish* repeat *yet with a pleasing sorcery this could charm*; and *yet with —— this could* before *excite* and *arm*.

l. 569. *As with*, &c. In full: *as it would arm the breast with triple steel*.

l. 571. *On bold adventure,* and *to discover,* &c. form adverbial adjuncts of *bend.*

l. 572. Before *if* repeat *to discover.*

l. 575. *Four infernal rivers.* The ancient Greeks imagined the life of the departed in the unseen world to be a shadowy and joyless reflection of the life of the present. Accordingly they assigned to the unseen region of souls various features of any ordinary landscape, —rocks, plains, meadows, rivers, trees, houses—or, at any rate, a house (that of Hades). They seemed to have formed a more definite idea of the rivers than of any other feature of this subterranean abode, and named five, which are here mentioned by Milton with epithets which explain the meaning of the significant Greek names. *Styx* is derived from *stygeo* (I hate); Acheron from *achos* (grief), and *rheo* (flow); *Cocytus,* from *cocyo* (I bewail); *Phlegethon* or *Pyriphlegethon,* from *pyr* (fire), and *phlegetho* (blaze); and *Lethe* is the word *lethe* (forgetfulness). According to Homer (*Od.* x. 513), Pyriphlegethon and Cocytus, of which Styx was a branch, discharged their streams into Acheron. We also sometimes find Styx, or Acheron, spoken of as being or forming a pool or marsh. The following passages of Virgil should be compared:—*Æn.* VI. 106:

> "Quando hic inferni janua regis
> Dicitur, et tenebrosa palus Acheronte refuso."

VI. 438:

> "Tristique palus inamabilis unda,
> Alligat, et novies Styx interfusa coercet."

VI. 549:

> "Mœnia lata videt, triplici circumdata muro;
> Quæ rapidus flammis ambit torrentibus amnis
> Tartareus Phlegethon, torquetque sonantia saxa."

VI. 713:

> "Animæ, quibus altera fato
> Corpora debentur, Lethæi ad fluminis undam
> Securos latices et longa oblivia potant."

In the conception of the early Greeks the abode or realm of Hades was quite distinct from the profounder abyss of Tartarus, in which the Titans were imprisoned by Zeus. To the Homeric Greek the earth was a round flat disc, of considerable thickness, within which was the realm of Hades, while heaven was the solid vault of the sky above the earth, and Tartarus a corresponding inverted hemisphere beneath. In later times Tartarus was represented as a portion of the realm of Hades.

l. 584. *Her watery labyrinth.* Milton seems here to have applied to Lethe Virgil's description of Styx, *novies interfusa.* Supply *he* before *who*, and repeat *whereof he who drinks* before forgets in *l.* 586. The clause *whereof—pain* is an adjective clause attached to *Lethe.* (*Gr.* 408. *An.* 77.)

l. 589. *Which on firm land thaws not,* [*which*] *gathers heap, and* [*which*] *seems* [*the*] *ruin of* [*some*] *ancient pile,* are three adjective clauses attached to *hail.*

l. 591. After *ice* supply the verb *lies.*

l. 592. *As that Serbonian bog,* &c., supply the predicate *was profound.* The morass here spoken of was situated between the eastern angle of the Delta of Egypt and Mount Casius. It was anciently much larger than at present, and formed the limit of Egypt towards the north-east.

l. 594. Milton here adopts the statement of Diodorus Siculus (I. 30), who says that the army which Darius Ochus was leading to the conquest of Egypt, was annihilated in this morass. But as we find that this same army afterwards took some Egyptian towns, this statement must be regarded as an exaggeration.

l. 595. *Frore* means *frosty.* (Compare the German past participle *gefroren.*) So Virgil, *Georg.* I. 93. "Boreæ penetrabile frigus adurat."

l. 600. We shall get the simplest construction if we supply *they are brought* before *from beds,* &c. *Hurried* must be attached grammatically to *they.* Compare Shakspere, *Measure for Measure,* Act III. Scene 1:—

"Ay, but to die, and go we know not where,
To lie in cold obstruction, and to rot;
This sensible warm motion to become
A kneaded clod, and the delighted spirit
To bathe in fiery floods, or to reside
In thrilling regions of thick-ribbed ice;
To be imprisoned in the viewless winds,
And blown with restless violence round about
The pendant world," &c.

l. 604. *Sound,* i. e., *strait* or *channel.*

l. 606. First leave out *and struggle,* and then repeat the sentence, substituting *struggle* for *wish.*

l. 609. *And so near the brink.* The grammatical connection of this with what precedes is very loose. The best way is to supply *they being,* so as to make a nominative absolute, which may be attached as an adverbial adjunct to the predicates *wish* and *struggle.*

l. 611. *Medusa.* Homer speaks of only one Gorgon, who was one of the terrible phantoms of Hades (*Od.* xi. 633). Hesiod names three, of whom Medusa was one. The Argive hero Perseus was fabled to have cut off the head of Medusa while she was asleep, making use of a mirror, to avoid looking directly at the monster, the sight of whose face turned all beholders to stone. He presented the head to Athene, who fixed it in her breastplate or shield.

l. 613. *Wight* is a person or being. We find the corresponding word, *wicht*, in the German *Bösewicht*.

l. 614. Various stories were told of the punishment of Tantalus in the lower world, and of the offence for which he suffered. The popular one was, that in order to test the discrimination of the gods he invited them to a repast, and cut his son Pelops in pieces, which he boiled and placed before them. Demeter, who was absorbed in grief for the loss of her daughter, incautiously ate one of the shoulders. The parts were put together again, and revivified by Hermes, and Demeter supplied an ivory shoulder in place of what she had consumed. Another account was, that being admitted to the society of the gods, he divulged their secrets. As to his punishment, some stories represented a huge rock to be perpetually impending over him and threatening to crush him; others spoke of his being tormented with perpetual thirst, and plunged in a lake, the waters of which fled from his lips when he attempted to taste them; or of his seeing delicious fruits hanging within reach, which were wafted away when he attempted to pluck them. His name has given us the verb *tantalize*.

l. 617. Before *found* repeat *the adventurous bands*.

l. 621. Repeat *over* with each of these nouns. We get a succession of adverbial adjuncts of the predicate *passed*

l. 622. *Which God—good.* An adjective clause, qualifying *universe*. *Evil* and *good* form the complements of the predicate *created*.

l. 624. Repeat *where* before *death* and *nature*. We thus get three other adjective clauses attached to *universe*. (*Gr.* 408 *An.* 77.)

l. 625. Repeat *things* with each of the adjectives. *Worse than*, &c. In full: *worse than fables yet have feigned* [*things bad*], *or* [*than*] *fear has conceived* [*things bad*]. Two adverbial clauses qualifying *worse*. *Than* in each case qualifies *bad* understood. (*Gr.* 549 &c., and note, p. 141. *An.* 150; note, p. 42.)

l. 628. Compare Virgil, *Æn.* VI. 287:—

"Bellua Lernæ,
Horrendum stridens, flammisque armata Chimæra,
Gorgones, Harpyiæque."

Also, *l.* 576:—

"Quinquaginta atris immanis hiatibus hydra."

The nine heads of the monstrous water-serpent (Hydra), slain by Hercules, are multiplied by Virgil into fifty.

Chimæra. This fire-breathing monster, slain by Bellerophon, is described by Homer as having the fore part of its body like a lion, the hinder part like a dragon, and the middle like a goat.

l. 630. *Inflamed* is an attributive adjunct of the subject *Satan.* Repeat the subject with each of the verbs that follow.

l. 636. Between *as* and *when* insert *a fleet seems.* The whole compound adverbial clause is co-ordinate with the *so* which qualifies *seemed*, in *l.* 642. The subordinate clause, *when—drugs*, is attached to the verb *seems* understood.

l. 637. *Hangs in the clouds.* Most persons must have noticed the seeming elevation of the line of the horizon when the sea is viewed from a height.

l. 639. Ternate and Tidore are two of the Moluccas.

l. 640. *They—pole.* This sentence must be taken as a parenthesis. It has no grammatical connexion with what precedes. *Trading* means "flowing in a regular tread or track." In old English writers the word *trade* does not at all necessarily imply *commerce.* Spenser speaks of the *trade* (i. e. *track*) of a wild beast. Udall speaks of the Jews being *in the right trade of religion.* In the Indian Ocean there is a strong southerly current, known as the Mozambique current, running first from east to west past the northern extremity of Madagascar, and then deflected southwards by the coast of Africa. Cape Corrientes (the *currents*) takes its name from it. The trade *wind* of the Indian Ocean would not carry a vessel southwards, but rather to the north of west, and the Monsoons, north of the equator, blow in different seasons in opposite directions. Moreover, Milton would hardly speak of a wind as a *flood.*

l. 642. *Stemming.* That is, directing the *stem* or *prow* of the vessel.

l. 645. Before *the gates* supply *were* or else *appear.*

l. 650. Repeat *the one seemed before fair.* *Foul* may be taken as complement of *ended.* Repeat *in* before *a serpent.* We thus get an adverbial adjunct of *ended.* This description of Sin is made up of that of Echidna, in Hesiod, half nymph and half serpent, and that of Scylla in Ovid's "Metamorphoses," who, by the jealousy of Circe, was changed from a beautiful nymph into a monster half woman, half fish, with dogs howling around her.

l. 654. *Cry* means a *pack*. Shakspere speaks of a *cry of curs*.

l. 655. *Cerberean*. (See note on *l.* 575.) As Hades had a *house* in the lower world, so he was provided with a *house-dog*, in the form of the three-headed Cerberus.

l. 659. After *abhorred* supply *creatures* or *hounds*. *Trinacria* was an ancient name of Sicily. *Than these*. In full: *than these* [*were abhorred*.]

l. 665. Aristophanes, in his comedy the "Clouds," mentions the superstition that the moon could be removed from the sky by the incantation of witches. Virgil (*Æn.* I. 642) calls eclipses of the sun *labores solis*.

l. 666. *The other shape*. This sentence is incomplete; there is no verb to which shape can be the subject. The simplest way is to leave out the *it* in *l.* 670.

This description of Death is justly celebrated as one of the grandest in the whole poem.

l. 667. *If shape—either*. This adverbial clause must be attached to the predicate of a sentence supplied, *I say shape*, or something of the kind. The whole must be treated as a parenthesis.

l. 667. *That shape had none—limb*. The use of *or* compels us to separate this for analysis into three sentences:—*that shape had none distinguishable in member; that shape had none distinguishable in joint; that shape had none distinguishable in limb*. All three are adjective clauses qualifying the subject *it*.

l. 669. In full: *or if it might be called substance that seemed shadow*.

l. 670. *For each seemed either*. This clause is but loosely connected with what precedes. It is inserted as though the preceding sentence were, *it was doubtful whether the shape should be called substance or shadow*, to the predicate of which it might then be attached.

As night [*is black*]. An adverbial clause of degree qualifying *black*. The connective adverb *as* qualifies the adjective *black* understood.

l. 671. In full: *Fierce* [*it stood*] *as ten furies* [*are fierce*], *terrible* [*it stood*] *as hell* [*is terrible*.]

l. 672 *What seemed his head*. An adjective clause used substantively. (*Gr.* 148.)

l. 675. *As fast.* That is, *equally fast.* The adverb *onwara* must be attached to the verb *came.*

l. 676. *As* is here used in the sense of *while.*

l. 677. *What this might be.* A substantive clause, the object of *admired.* *What* is the complement of the verb of incomplete predication *might be.* (Compare *Gr.* 495. *An.* 99.)

l. 678. *God and His Son,* &c. This must be taken as the rhetorical equivalent of *he valued no created thing in the least degree except God and His Son.* Where the adverbial expression *except God and His Son* qualifies and limits the adjective of quantity *no.*

l. 679. *Nor shunned.* Repeat the whole of the preceding sentence with the substitution of *shunned,* for *valued in any degree.*

l. 682. Supply *thou art* before *grim.* First leave out *and what,* and then repeat the whole, substituting *what* for *whence.*

l. 685. *That be assured* is a parenthetical sentence. It would be more correct to say *Of that be assured.*

l. 691. Before *in proud* repeat *who.*

l. 692. *The third part.* (Compare Rev. xii. 3, 4.) "Behold a great red dragon, and his tail drew the third part of the stars of heaven, and cast them to the earth."

Conjured is used in the sense of the Latin *conjurati,* sworn together, banded together by an oath.

l. 693. *For which,* &c. This, though an adjective clause in form, does not attach itself to any particular word in what precedes. Treat *for which* as equivalent to *and for this.*

l. 698. *Where I reign king.* In its present form this must be treated as an adverbial sentence, co-ordinate with the adverb *here.* We should get the relation of the ideas more exactly if we substituted *in this place in which I reign king.*

And to enrage, &c. In full: *and where, I tell thee to enrage thee more, that I reign thy lord and king.* Supply *go* before *back.*

l. 705. Repeat *the grisly terror* before *grew.*

l. 710. *In the Arctic sky.* It is only when the celestial sphere is divided into a northern and a southern half by the ecliptic that the greater part of the constellation of Ophiuchus is in the northern portion. The equator leaves the greater part in the southern. Before *from* repeat *that.*

l. 711. Among the prodigies portending the death of Cæsar, and the consequent civil war, Virgil mentions (*Georg.* I. 488)—

Nec diri toties arsere cometæ.

l. 714. *As when—mid air.* An adverbial clause qualifying *such.* After *as* supply *the frown is,* to the predicate of which the clause *when two,* &c., is attached.

l. 715. *Rattling* forms a complement to the predicate *come.*

l. 716. Before *then* repeat *when two black clouds.*

Front to front. An adverbial expression, partaking of the nature of a nominative absolute.

l. 718. *To join,* &c. This forms an attributive adjunct to *signal.* (*Gr.* 362, 4. *An.* 20, 4.)

l. 719. *That—frown.* An adverbial clause qualifying *so.* *That* is itself a connective adverb qualifying *grew.* (*Gr.* 528, 529. *An.* 133, 134.)

l. 721. *But* is here a preposition. *But once* (i. e. *one time*) *more* is an adverbial phrase qualifying and limiting *never.*

l. 726. After *and* repeat *if the snaky sorceress that sat—they had not.*

l. 729. *To bend,* &c. An adverbial adjunct of *possesses.*

l. 730. In full: *and knowest thou for whom thou bendest that mortal dart against thy father's head?*

l. 731. Before *for him* repeat *thou bendest that—head.*

l. 734. In analysis leave out the repetition *his wrath.*

l. 731. Repeat the clause *that my—my son* in each of the sentences, *so strange* [*is*] *thy outcry,* and *thy words so strange thou interposest.* It qualifies the adverb *so* in each case. (*Gr.* 528 *An.* 133.)

l. 741. Before *why* repeat *till first I know of thee.*

l. 743. Before *that phantasm* repeat *till first I know of thee why thou.* The clauses beginning with *why* are substantive clauses, the objects of the verb *know.*

l. 745. *Than him and thee.* These objective cases can only be explained by filling up the clause thus:—*than I see thee and him detestable.* The clause is adverbial, and qualifies *more.* (*Gr.* 549, &c.; note on p. 166. *An.* 149, &c.; note, p. 42.)

l. 749. The whole compound clause, *when at the—I sprung,* is in the adverbial relation to *deemed.*

l. 753. Repeat *when* before *dim.* Take the words thus:—*when thine eyes, dim and dizzy, swum in darkness.*

l. 754. The adverbial clauses, *while thy—forth,* and *till—I sprung,* qualify *swum.*

l. 756. *Likest,* &c., *shining,* &c., and *a goddess armed,* are all attributive adjuncts of *I.* This whole description is, of course, an adaptation of the Greek legend of the birth of Minerva from the head of Jupiter. The rest of the passage is based upon the idea expressed in James i. 15: "Then when lust hath conceived, it bringeth forth sin; and sin, when it is finished, bringeth forth death."

l. 806. *But* is here a preposition governing the compound substantive clause *that he knows—shall be*, with which it forms an adverbial adjunct to *would devour.*

He knows, &c. Expand thus:—*he knows that his end is involved with mine.*

l. 813. Before *tempered* insert *they are.*

l. 814. *Save he*, &c. This should be *save him*, &c., unless *save* be regarded as an adjective, the same as *safe*, forming a nominative absolute with the substantive that follows. Anyhow the whole phrase *save—above* is in the adverbial relation to *none*, which it qualifies and defines. (*Gr.* 283.)

l. 817. The adverbial clause *since thou—unthought of* qualifies the predicate of a clause understood, *I call thee daughter*, or something equivalent.

l. 822. After *but* repeat *know that I come.*

l. 830. *A place foretold should be.* We can only make grammar of this by expanding it thus:—*a place which it was foretold should be*, where the entire clause *which it was—be*, is an adjective clause qualifying place, while the secondary clause, *which should be*, is a substantive clause, in apposition to *it*, the subject of *was foretold.* If a demonstrative pronoun were used instead of a relative, we could insert the conjunction *that*:—*it was foretold that that should be.* This is always the best way of testing the construction of an involved clause containing a relative.

l. 833. *And therein*, &c. The construction is obscure. If *and* be retained, we must repeat after it, *to search with wandering quest a race of upstart creatures therein placed*, &c.

l. 835. The compound clause, *though* [*they are*] *more removed—broils*, qualifies *placed.*

l. 837. In full: *I haste to know whether this be now designed, or whether aught were more secret than this* [*is secret*] *be now designed.*

l. 840. *Where thou—odours.* A compound adjective clause qualifying *place.* Before *up* repeat *where thou and Death shall.*

l. 842. *Buxom* here has its original meaning *yielding.* It is derived from the Anglo-Saxan *bugan*, to bend or yield, and answers to the German *biegsam.* It afterwards came to mean *plump and soft*, and also *compliant.*

l. 855. *To be o'ermatched*, &c., forms an adverbial adjunct to *fearless*.

l. 857. The adjective clauses *who hates me*, and *who hath—seal*, qualify the substantive pronoun *his*. (*Gr.* 141.)

l. 875. *But herself* forms an adverbial adjunct of *not all*, which is used as equivalent to *none of*.

l. 877. The notion of turning the *wards* is inaccurate. The wards belong to the lock, not to the key.

l. 882. *That shook*, &c., is an adjective clause qualifying *thunder*.

l. 885. *That with—array*. An adverbial clause denoting consequence, attached to the predicate *stood*. *That* is itself a connective adverb qualifying *pass*. (*Gr.* 528. *An.* 133.)

l. 892. After *ocean* repeat *appears*.

l. 893. *Where length—are lost*, is an adjective clause qualifying *ocean*. *Height* is here used, like the Latin *altitudo*, in the sense of *depth*.

l. 894. The word *Chaos* means *empty space*, and that was the earliest conception of what preceded the existence of the material universe. Hesiod (*Theogon.* 116) says that Chaos existed first, then the Earth and Tartarus, and Eros, that is, the generative principle. Of Chaos were born or produced Erebus (darkness or gloom) and Night. Night and Erebus were the parents of Æther (bright or blazing sky) and Day; and Earth gave birth to Heaven. Chaos afterwards came to signify the aggregate of confused material elements out of which the universe was formed. Some spoke of *Night* as the origin of all things. Thus in one of the Orphic hymns Night is addressed as the parent of gods, men, and all things The philosopher Thales assumed *water* to be the origin of all things, that is, he conceived the primal elemental matter to be homogeneous and fluid, but capable of passing into the various material forms of the visible universe. Anaximenes considered *air* to be the primary form of matter. Anaximander spoke of it more indefinitely as *the infinite*, which he appears to have regarded as a mixture of heterogeneous but unchangeable elements, which were arranged and organised by the force of heat and cold and the affinities of the various particles. Anaxagoras was the first who arrived at the noble conception that *intelligence* was the motive power which brought order into the chaotic mass. His theory was expressed in the dictum, "All things were mixed up together; then intelligence arranged them." Empedocles of Agrigentum first laid down the doctrine that the primary matter of the universe consisted of the four elements, fire, air, earth, and water, which were fashioned into the various objects of visible nature by the opposite motive powers of attraction and repulsion (or love and hate). Democritus of Abdera introduced the conception that the primary matter of the universe consisted of *atoms*, and this theory was adopted and developed by Epicurus. Milton seems to have had before him a notable passage in Ovid (*Metam.* I. 5, &c.) :—

"Ante mare et terras et quod tegit omnia cœlum,
Unus erat toto naturæ vultus in orbe,
Quem dixere Chaos, rudis indigestaque moles;
Nec quidquam nisi pondus iners; congestaque eodem
Non bene junctarum discordia semina rerum.

* * * * *

"Sic erat instabilis tellus, innabilis unda,
Lucis egens aër; nulli sua forma manebat,
Obstabatque aliis aliud; quia corpore in uno
Frigida pugnabant calidis, humentia siccis,
Mollia cum duris, sine pondere habentia pondus.
Hanc Deus et melior litem Natura diremit."

But those among the ancients who accepted the idea of intelligence or Divine power bringing chaos into order, still regarded the process as nothing more than an application of previously-existing and unalterable forces. It is only that philosophy which has been taught by Revelation which has attained to an apprehension of the grand fact of *creation*, and traces in the laws and forces of nature the expression of the *will* and *wisdom* of that Infinite Intelligence whose "eternal power and Godhead are understood by the things that are made." Compare with Milton's magnificent, but semi-Pagan description, the first chapter of Genesis.

l. 901. *Of each his faction.* This attempt to make a possessive of *each* is not admissible. It should be *each around the flag of his faction.* (See *Gr.* 73, note.)

l. 902. As the conjunction *or* does not here involve an alternative, of which only one case can be true, all these adjectives may be taken as co-ordinate attributive adjuncts of *they.*

l. 903. In full: *unnumbered as the sands of Barca* [*are unnumbered*], *or* [*unnumbered as the sands of*] *Cyrene's torrid soil* [*are unnumbered.*]

l. 905. *Levied* (from *levare*) here means raised up.

l. 906. *To whom these most adhere.* An adjective clause qualifying the *he* that follows.

l. 912. In full: *not composed (mixed) of sea, and not composed of shore, and not composed of air, and not composed of fire, but composed confusedly of all these in their pregnant causes.* The *and* in *l.* 214 is superfluous, and prevents the proper connection of the adjective clause *which—worlds* with *these*.

l. 917. In analysis leave out the repetition *into this wild abyss*.

Take *the wary fiend stood on the brink of hell* as a separate sentence, and connect *into this wild abyss*, &c., only with *look'd;* otherwise *stood* must be altered to *standing*, and *and* must be omitted.

l. 922. After *than* insert *the ear is pealed.*

l. 924. *Or less than.* In full: *or was his ear less pealed than the ear would be pealed if this frame*, &c.

l. 930. After *as* supply *he would ride. Chair* is the same as *chaise* or *car.*

l. 639. In full: *that fury being quenched in a boggy syrtis which was not sea and which was not good dry land.*

l. 942. *Behoves*, &c. A very awkward, not to say incorrect expression. Read *it behoves him now to use both oar and sail.* This was a proverbial expression in Latin. Thus Cicero (*Tusc.* III. 11) says:—*Tetra enim res est misera, detestabilis, omni contentione, velis, ut ita dicam, remisque fugienda.*

l. 943. After *as* supply *oar and sail are needed.*

l. 945. The Arimaspians were a fabulous one-eyed race, dwelling in Scythia, ever seeking to steal the gold which was guarded by the gryphons, creatures half lion, half eagle.

l. 944. *Or* may here be taken as having much the same sense as *and: o'er hill*, and *o'er moory dale* are co-ordinate adverbial adjuncts of *pursues.* The whole adverbial clause *as when—gold* is attached to the adverb *so*, which qualifies *eagerly.*

l. 948. Respecting the force of *or* see note on *l.* 944.

l. 950. Each of these verbs makes a separate sentence. Supply the subject *the fiend* with each.

l. 956. First leave out *or spirit*, and then repeat the whole sentence, substituting *spirit* for *power. Whatever power* had better be treated, for the purpose of analysis, as equivalent to *any power which.*

l. 959. *When straight—deep.* An adverbial clause qualifying *plies. Behold* is the rhetorical equivalent of *there appeared.*

l. 965. Demogorgon was not a being known to the classical

mythologists. It was a mysterious and awful power, terrible even to gods, invoked in magical incantations. Later writers, such as Lucan (VI. 744), and Statius (*Theb.* IV. 514), refer to it. After *Rumour* supply *stood*.

l. 971. *With purpose*, &c., must be taken as an attributive adjunct of *spy*.

l. 977. *If some—lately.* An adverbial clause attached to *travel*.

l. 981. *Directed.* That is, *my course being directed*, a nominative absolute, forming an adverbial adjunct of *brings*.

l. 988. *Anarch.* This is rather a bold coinage. *Anarchy* is the *absence of government*. An *anarch holding sway* over chaos, is therefore a self-contradictory conception.

l. 990. This can only be reduced within the rules of analysis by substituting *I know thee, I know who thou art*.

l. 991. Before *that* insert *thou art*.

l. 992. *Though* [*thou wast*] *overthrown*. An adverbial clause of concession attached to *made*.

l. 999. *If all—Night.* An adverbial clause attached to *keep*:—*if all* [*that*] *I can* [*do*] *will serve so to defend that little which is left, encroached on*, &c.

l. 1003. After *beneath* supply *encroached on my frontiers:* and repeat the same predicate in the next sentence.

l. 1011. *That now—shore.* This may be treated as an adverbial clause qualifying the adjective *glad*. We should get much the same sense if we substituted *because* for *that*.

l. 1017. After *than* insert *Argo was endangered*. Argo was the famous ship in which Jason and his companions, the Argonauts, sailed to fetch the golden fleece from Colchis.

l. 1018. *The justling rocks.* These were the Cyaneæ or Symplegades, two rocks at the entrance of the Thracian Bosphorus, which are near to each other, and as a ship threads its way up the channel seem alternately to approach to and to recede from one another. Hence the fable that they were moveable, and closed upon and crushed any ship that attempted to sail between them.

l. 1020. *Charybdis.* This celebrated whirlpool (called now the Galofaro) is in the Sicilian Straits, near Messina. Its dangers were not altogether imaginary, though very much exaggerated by the timid navigators of ancient times. Milton seems here to speak of Scylla as another whirlpool. This is a mistake. Scylla or Scyllæum was a rocky promontory on the Italian coast, about fifteen miles N.

of Rhegium, forming two small bays, one on each side. There is absolutely no danger in sailing past it, and it is difficult to understand how it could ever have been regarded as a perilous obstacle. This rock was represented by the mythologists as the abode of the monster Scylla (*l.* 660). In Homer (*Od.* XII. 85), Scylla is described as a monster with twelve misshapen feet, six long necks, supporting frightful heads, in the mouth of each of which were three rows of teeth full of black death. The later form of the legend is mentioned in the note on *l.* 660.

l. 1023. *He once past.* A nominative absolute, forming an adverbial adjunct to *paved.*

l. 1032. Before *whom* supply the antecedent *those.*

l. 1039. As a broken foe [would retire] from her outmost works.

l. 1041. *That Satan,* &c. This intricate adverbial clause, which ends at *l.* 1053, is attached to the predicate *begins* in each of the preceding sentences.

l. 1042. *Wafts* is here intransitive, equivalent to *floats.*

l. 1043. *Holds the port* is a translation of the Latin phrase *occupat portum.*

l. 1046. *Weighs* is a rendering of the Latin *librat*, which rather means *balances. At leisure,* &c., forms an adverbial adjunct to *weighs. To behold,* &c., is an attributive adjunct to *leisure.*

l. 1048. In full: *undetermined whether it be square or whether it be round.*

l. 1052. *As a star,* &c. Insert the predicate understood *is big.*

A LIST OF WORDS USED IN OBSOLETE OR UNUSUAL SENSES.

Access (*accessus, accedo*), way by which approach may be made. (*l.* 130.)
Acclaim (*acclamare*), a shout raised at anything. (*l.* 520.)
Admire (*admirari*), to wonder. (*l.* 678.)
Adverse (*adversus*), contrary to our proper nature. (*l.* 77.)
Afflicting (*affligo*), dashing against. (*l.* 166.)
Ambrosial (ἀμβροσία 'the food of the gods,' from ἄμβροτος 'immortal,') like ambrosia. (*l.* 245.)
Antagonist (ἀνταγωνιστής), one capable of wrestling against an adversary. (*l.* 509.)
Atlantean, like those of Atlas. Atlas was a mythological personage, represented as bearing up the pillars which keep heaven and earth asunder, or as supporting the heavens on his shoulders. His name was subsequently localized in the mountain chain in the north-west of Africa. (*l.* 306.)
Awful, full of awe—*i.e.*, full of reverential respect.

Cease (*cessare*), to hesitate or delay. (*l.* 159.)
Chair (*carrus*), chariot. (*l.* 930.)
Charm, *s.* (*carmen*), a spell or incantation. (*l.* 266.)
Charm, *v.*, to put under a spell, to bewitch or beguile. (*l.* 566.)
Compose (*componĕre*), to arrange or put together, to bring into good order. (*l.* 280.)
Composed (*compositus*), made up. (*l.* 111.)
Compulsion (*compellĕre*), force exerted in driving. (*l.* 80.)
Confine (*confinis*), to have the same boundary with. (*l.* 977.)
Conjecture (*conjectura, conjicio*), anticipation as to the result of a course of action.
Conjured (*conjurare*), bound together by oath. (*l.* 693.)

Dash, to overthrow. (*l.* 114.)
Deform, *adj.* (*deformis*), shapeless, hideous. (*l.* 706.)

Demur (*demorari*), doubt, hesitation. (*l.* 431.)
Descent (*descendĕre*), depth to which we have fallen. (*l.* 14.)
Determine (*de, terminus*), to settle one's position and limits. (*l.* 330.)
Dimension (*dimensio, dimetiri*), extent that admits of being measured. (*l.* 893.)

Element (*elementa*, 'first principles'), a primary or simple substance. According to the notions held in Milton's time, the term *elements* was especially applied to fire, air, earth, and water. The *element* of any living creature is that one of these four, in or on which it naturally lives. (*l.* 275.)
Empyreal (ἔμπυρος), dwelling in the region of fire, heavenly. See *Ethereal* (*l.* 431). 'The empyrean' (*l.* 771), means 'heaven.'
Entertain, to amuse or beguile. (*l.* 526.)
Errand, in Anglo-Saxon, *ærend*. Not from *errare*.
Essential (*essentia*, modern Latin derivative from *esse*), being, nature, 'This essential.' (*l.* 97.)
Ethereal (*æthereus*, αἰθήρ 'blazing heat'), belonging to the region of æther—*i.e.*, to heaven. By *æther*, the ancients understood the upper, pure, glowing air beyond the region of mists and clouds (ἀήρ); a rare and fiery medium, in which the heavenly bodies moved. (*l.* 311, 978.)
Evasion (*evasio, evadĕre*), power of making one's way out. (*l.* 411.)
Event (*eventus, evenio*), the result of a course of action. (*l.* 82.)
Excellence (*excellĕre*), superiority in any quality, not merely superiority in goodness.
Excursion (*ex, currĕre*), a hasty sally. (*l.* 396.)
Exempt (*eximĕre* 'to take out'), removed to a distance, released or delivered. (*l.* 318.)

Fact (*factum*), feat. *French*, 'fait.' (*l.* 124.)
Fall, to happen (*l.* 203). Compare *accidere* (from *ad* and *cadĕre* 'to fall').
Fame (*fama*), report. (*l*, 346.)
Fatal (*fatalis, fatum*), established by fate. (*l.* 104.)
Forgetful, causing forgetfulness. (*l.* 74.)
Forlorn, lost. *German*, 'verloren.' (*l.* 615.)
Fraught, another form of the past participle of *freight*. (*l.* 715.)
Fury (*furor*), madness. (*l.* 728.)

Horrent (*horrēre*), bristling. (*l.* 513.)
Horrid (*horridus*), bristling. (*l.* 710.)

Imaginations (*imago, imaginatio*), plans, designs.
Impaled (*in, palus*, 'a stake'), enclosed. The word signifies properly, 'enclosed with stakes,' or 'fixed on a stake.' (*l.* 647.)
Impendent (*in, pendĕre*), hanging over us. (*l.* 177.)
Impotence (*impotentia, in, potens*) want of self-control. (*l.* 156.)

Incensed (*incendĕre*), kindled, fired. (*l.* 707.)
Industrious (*industria*), bending one's energies towards some end. (*l.* 116.) *Ex industria*, 'of set purpose.'
Inflame (*inflammare*), to blaze. (*l.* 581.)
Instinct (*instinguĕre*), goaded on, incited, or impelled. (*l.* 937.)
Intellectual (*intelligĕre*), possessed of understanding. (*l.* 147.)
Intend (*in*, *tendĕre*), to direct the mind to any subject. (*l.* 457.)
Involve (*involvĕre*), to wrap up. (*l.* 384.)

Labouring (*laborare*), suffering disaster. (*l.* 665.)

Mansion (*mansio*, *manēre*), a dwelling-place. (*l.* 462.)

Need (*l.* 413), used apparently as an adjective; 'to have need,' being equivalent to the German phrase, 'nöthig haben.'

Obdured (*obdurare*), hardened. (*l.* 568.)
Obscure (*obscurus*), dark, not easily seen. (*l.* 132.)
O'erwatched, kept awake for an unusual or excessive length of time. (*l.* 288.)
Ominous (*omen*, *ominosus*), full of threatenings of disaster. 'Ominous conjecture' = anticipation of disaster.
Opinion (*opinio*), estimation, judgment. (*l.* 471.)

Palpable (*palpare*), that may be felt. 'The palpable obscure' = darkness that may be felt.
Partial (*pars*), taken up by a few only. (*l.* 552.)
Passion (*passio*, *patior*), suffering, the being affected by anything. The opposite of this is apathy. (*l.* 564.)
Patience (*patientia*), power of endurance. (*l.* 569.)
Pitch, the highest point (*l.* 772). *Pitch* is of the same origin as *pike* and *spike*, and implies the acute angle formed by the meeting of two lines or surfaces in a point or edge. A *high-pitched roof* is a roof with a high *ridge*. Hence the idea of *elevation*, which is attached to the word *pitch*. *Picea*, 'the pitch-pine,' is so called from its form, and that of its leaves. The verbs *pick* and *peck* are connected with the radical notion of point.
Policy (πολιτεία), the action and life of a settled state. (*l.* 297.)
Possess (*possidēre*), seize upon. (*ll.* 365, 979.)
Presumptuous (*præsumĕre*), taking too soon, or before proper permission is given. (*l.* 522.) 'Presumptuous hope' = hope that is directed to its object too soon.
Pretence (*prætendĕre*, 'to stretch in front'), a claim put forwards. (*l.* 825.)
Prime (*primus*), foremost. (*l.* 423.)
Process (*processus*, *procedĕre*), advance. (*l.* 297.)
Prohibit (*prohibĕre*), to stop. (*l.* 437.)
Prone (*pronus*), bending low. (*l.* 478.)

Rare (*rarus*), thinly scattered; the opposite of *dense*. (*l.* 948.)
Redounding (*redundare*), overflowing, spreading in billows beyond the proper limits. (*l.* 889.)
Reluctance (*reluctare*, 'to struggle against'), obstinate resistance. (*l.* 337.)
Remit (*remittere*), relax. (*l.* 210.)
Revolutions (*revolutio*), revolving periods. (*l.* 597.)
Ruinous (*ruina*, *ruo*), crashing, as when a building falls suddenly. (*l.* 921.)

Scope (*σκοπός*), a mark aimed at. (*l.* 127.)
Scowl, threaten with a scowling look. (*l.* 491.)
Specious (*species*, *speciosus*), having a noble or fair appearance. (*l.* 484.)
Starve, to cause to perish by cold. The word is not necessarily connected with the idea of hunger. *German*, 'sterben.'
Station (*statio*), a body of troops on guard. (*l.* 412.)
Stygian, hellish. See note on *l.* 575. (*l.* 506.)
Sublime (*sublimis*), raised aloft. (*l.* 528.)
Success (*succedĕre*), the result, good or bad, of a course of action. (*ll.* 9, 123.)
Suspense *adj.* (*suspensus*), in suspense. (*l.* 418.)
Synod (*σύνοδος*), assembly.

Tartarean, belonging to Tartarus—*i.e.*, hell. (*l.* 69).
Temper (*temperare*, 'to mix in due proportion'), constitution. (*ll.* 218, 276.)
Torrent (*torrēre*), scorching. (*l.* 581.)
Trading, flowing in a regular *tread* or tract. (*l.* 640.)

Uncouth (*Anglo-Saxon*, uncuð), unknown. (*ll.* 407, 827.)
Unessential, having no real being or substance. (*l.* 439.) See 'essential.'
Unexpert (*expertus*), inexperienced. (*l.* 52.)
Upright, bearing the body upwards.

Voluminous (*volumen*, *volvo*), having many rolls or folds. (*l.* 652.)
Voyage, journey. (*l.* 426). Compare the French *voyage*.

Waft (*instransitive*), to float on air, or any buoyant medium. (*l.* 1046.)
Wasteful, full of empty wastes. (*l.* 961.)
Weigh, to spread out in even balance. 'Weighs his spread wings.' (*l.* 1046.) An imitation of the Latin *librare*.

www.ingramcontent.com/pod-product-compliance
Lightning Source LLC
Chambersburg PA
CBHW020008030726
47500CB00002B/491

* 9 7 8 3 3 3 7 0 9 4 2 3 2 *